The Pirate's Island

For Jari & Tami

Hope You Enjoy

All My Very Best

09/16/2011

The Pirate's Island

Alan Del Monte

Library of Congress Control Number:		2011914478
ISBN:	Hardcover	978-1-4653-4761-9
	Softcover	978-1-4653-4760-2
	Ebook	978-1-4653-4762-6

This book was printed in the United States of America.

To order additional copies of this book, contact:
Xlibris Corporation
1-888-795-4274
www.Xlibris.com
Orders@Xlibris.com
100601

For Victoria
My Beloved

ACKNOWLEDGEMENTS

Pat Cucuzza: For being my friend and traveling every step of the way with me. And there were many.

Kim Sekelsky: For believing in me and pushing me.

Arthur Shultz: For encouraging and spurring me on.

Meg Russell Rideout: For graphic mastery and so much help.

Betsy Kan: For eagle eyes, patience and amazing attention to detail.

The Alan Del Monte Salon Staff: My daytime family. You showed up when it meant the most.

Special thanks to Bishop Jay Ramirez: My spiritual guide, my mentor and my friend.

To all of you who have been so kind and understanding during my darkest hour. May God bless you all.

CHAPTER ONE

No one could remember a wedding coming together this fast. Certainly, not a wedding of this magnitude. When the family reached home, late on the evening of the Street Festival in New Haven, Sam asked Martha to meet him on the porch. He put the children to bed and went down to sit with a waiting Martha who was enjoying the moonlight overlooking Wolf Harbor. Sam walked over to her, took her by the hands and raised her to her feet.

"The world is changing before our very eyes," he began. "The whole world is at war and we can no longer feel safe, not even here." The specter of the Skull and Bones, right down the road in New Haven, never left his consciousness. "Violent crime is on the rise," he continued, "and the events of the last two weeks have made me aware how precious the time is that we do have. The only thing I know for sure, Martha Frost, is that I want to change your last name to Tyler, and the sooner the better. I'd marry you right now, but that would cause any number of problems. We do have to do it properly, but fast. What do you say?"

Martha did not answer. Instead she threw her arms around Sam's neck and kissed him as hard as she could. "Oh yes, Sam, yes," she blurted out, releasing her lips but not her arms. "Samuel Tyler, you see these arms wrapped around you?" she asked. "You are the only person on this planet that will ever be able to release them."

Sam got the message.

On a bright Saturday morning in late July, Martha and Sam announced their wedding date: exactly two Saturdays from that very day. Of course, Aunt Clara was the first to hear the news, but it wasn't until Sam spoke to Reverend Foster at St. Peter's Episcopal Church to clear that date with him, that he and Martha could make it official. The children exploded with glee when Sam told them, while Injun Jim simply shook his head and wondered, "How in tarnation were they ever going to pull this thing off?"

❋   ❋   ❋

The next two weeks were absolutely crazy with activity. Martha and Aunt Clara bonded together like true blood family as they feverishly orchestrated every detail. Indeed, they kept up a constant laughing, hugging, crying and praising the Lord for the way things came together. Martha took the children to Edward Malley's, the famous department store down in New Haven for their wedding attire, Martha's included. It was a wonderful treat for the children, as this was something they had been denied by the untimely death of their mother, Sally. Now Martha would be filling that void, providing all three children with the experience of shopping with mom. It also gave Martha the opportunity to introduce the children to her best friend, Elizabeth Childers, over a late lunch at the Taft hotel, directly across from the Yale campus.

Aunt Clara hired Wanda Loomis to take care of the catering, no small matter. Ella Mae Rucker and a number of her church ladies manned the telephones for the invites. Written invitations were out of the question. Injun Jim contacted some of his Gypsy friends who had a number of old circus tents in perfect repair, no questions asked, to cover Aunt Clara's lawn, where the reception was to be held. Off duty police officers from the neighboring towns volunteered to valet park the visitors' cars. Sergeant Matt D'Onofrio contacted a number of well known New Haven musicians, all professionals with big band experience, to supply the music. Matt would stand in as Sam's best man in honor of Ethan Taft whom Sam had been very fond of. Sam had to admit that the Sergeant was a not too distant second choice. That was comforting. Injun Jim had one more duty to perform. He was given the responsibility of chauffeuring Martha and Aunt Clara wherever they needed to go. He felt more alive during these two weeks than he had in a long, long time.

When Lizzy Childers, Martha's obvious choice as maid of honor, called to inquire if floral arrangements had been made, Martha and Aunt Clara were horror struck. Not only had they not been made, they had not even been thought of. Aunt Clara hunkered down with Lizzy and explained the layout so she could make all the arrangements. All the flowers were a gift from Peter and her. But they were not the only gift. Lizzy's family could not attend but their sizable monetary gift could.

CHAPTER TWO

Over two hundred guests showed up to celebrate the occasion. One thing was for sure; no one was going to miss this affair, nor the opportunity to be photographed with Sam, a real local American hero. In fact, many were calling Sam a national hero as he helped to thwart a group dedicated to sabotaging the American war effort. Even the President sent a representative up from Washington to pay homage and, of course, make a good showing for the locals to see. The Governor, many state dignitaries, the mayors of the neighboring towns and anybody who was anybody cleared their calendars, changed their plans and made darn sure they were not going to be the ones to miss out.

The press, reaching all the way back to New York City, most notably the *New York Times*, was determined they were not going to be robbed of the opportunity to trumpet the marriage of an American hero and America's favorite wartime novelist. Ellen Gold dragged her husband up from New York to the affair and even Sam's youngest cousin, Caroline Tyler, who worked at the clerical department for the FBI in Columbia, South Carolina, managed to attend.

Martha was radiant in her simple but elegant gown, made of creamy satin with its sweetheart neckline; it was the essence of class. Long sleeves ending in a point at the wrists, adorned with tiny satin buttons that crept from the wrists to the elbows, were the only concessions to decorations. Her veil, on the other hand, made up for the gown's simplicity. Consisting entirely of Brussels handmade lace, it fell from a crown of orange blossoms, touching the floor and stretching out behind the gown like a very long train. It was the "something old" in the bridal ensemble; Martha was the fourth generation of the Tyler brides to wear it. As the wedding march began, and Martha entered the church, there was a collective gasp from the guests at their first sight of her. She looked exquisite!

It was her coming out party. It occurred to her and Ellen that her picture and story would appear in two separate sections of the *Times*. The world was finally going to see just who this Martha Frost was. As Ellen Gold would so eloquently put it, "It doesn't get any better than that, Honey."

The church ceremony could best be described as relaxed traditional. The Templetons, the children's grandparents, contributed a harpist and a string quartet from Juilliard in New York City to play during the ceremony. No less than three sopranos from the Metropolitan Opera, also courtesy of the Templeton's, performed a special opening song. But, the final song of joyful celebration was performed by Ella Mae Rucker and her church choir. They nearly brought the house down. Martha and Sam floated down the aisle to receive their guests in front of the church.

The reception on Aunt Clara's lawn would become the social event of the year. With the war going on, and all the sacrifices people were making, this was a welcome relief. Even though short-lived, it provided the locals with something to talk about for some time. As the locals would say, "It was just what the doctor ordered." The music played, everyone danced and mingled, and a good amount of networking went on. Mayor Tinsley caused a minor sensation when he showed up with a new woman on his arm. The early assessment by the members of the crowd was that she was a little garish in appearance, but she managed to display a surprising grace as the day wore into evening. She and Aunt Clara seemed to get along just fine. That scored major points in her favor. Allison Tinsley was the only noticeable absentee, no matter how hard the mayor tried to downplay the fact that she was an obvious no-show. It was understood, by everyone who knew Allison, that she would rather consume a gallon of cyanide than be there to watch her man in the arms of this outsider who had stolen him away. But, to be perfectly honest, no one really missed Allison, the mayor included.

CHAPTER THREE

Aunt Clara and the children were waiting on the lawn as Sam and Martha drove up the driveway. Seven days had passed and they were now home from their honeymoon at Lake Placid. The couple managed to spend one day and evening in Manhattan to catch up with Cousin Ellen, and for Martha to do some last minute shopping for the children for the trip to Colombia, South Carolina. Cousin Caroline had convinced them that Fort Sumter and the surrounding area were something all the children should see. The local area was just reeking with good old fashioned southern hospitality and charm. Martha convinced Sam to schedule a layover in Washington, DC on their way down. Surprisingly, it was a place Martha had never been.

The family was so excited to see them, and Lilith, hardly able to contain herself, exploded into Martha's arms. Everyone hugged and held onto one another. Aunt Clara was the happiest of all. She had prayed that this would happen but never would allow herself the disappointment of wishing for too much if it never did happen. She was so happy for her nephew who had found love again. But it was for the children that she was the most pleased. Now they would know, finally, what real family was all about. Her joy was complete. Even Injun Jim showed uncharacteristic emotion. The significance of this scene was not lost on him. "Things are certainly going to be different around here," he thought. "Different, but better."

Martha and Sam walked across the lawn to Martha's new home to freshen up. The children stayed with Aunt Clara to prepare cold drinks and sandwiches on the porch. Injun Jim helped Sam carry the luggage. Martha had instructed Injun Jim to take three large boxes into Aunt Clara's house. The new couple quickly washed up, changed clothes and joined the others on Aunt Clara's porch overlooking Wolf Harbor. Everyone wanted to know all the details about their time at Lake Placid. Martha noticed that Mary was unusually quiet. After a while she excused herself and asked Aunt Clara to join her. In the kitchen, Aunt Clara told Martha that one of Mary's friends, Heather Morrissey, had told Mary that she overheard her mother gossiping on the telephone to one of her lady friends about Martha. Her comments were not very kind. Basically, she called Martha an unwelcome opportunist who had no business interfering with Sam and the only acceptable mate for someone of his stature: none other than Allison Tinsley.

"That Morrissey girl is a real problem child," Aunt Clara informed her. "No wonder, with a mother like Millicent Morrissey. That Morrissey woman is a real town crier. She has her nose in everybody's business and always a comment, never a good one, mind you."

Martha leaned back against the sink to compose herself. She took a few deep breaths, a technique she had acquired for dealing with the fast-paced lunacy of Manhattan life.

"Sam and I spent long hours up at Lake Placid talking about our life together. He knows exactly where I stand and how much all of you mean to me. I think it would be a good idea for me to share all that with you and the children. And I think there's no better time to do it than now. But,

I would like to do that with just you and the children. I'm sure Sam will understand. It's very important to me that you and the children have the relationship with me that I so desire." She then led Aunt Clara back to the porch.

"I think it's time for our first family meeting," she informed the group. "Sam, would you mind if just this once, I spoke to Aunt Clara and the children, alone?"

"Not at all," said Sam. "I'm sure Injun Jim and I can busy ourselves over at the house. Just call when you want us back." With that he and Injun Jim got to their feet and made their way across the lawn.

There was definitely an air of apprehension as the group waited for Martha to begin. Martha took a few moments to gather her thoughts, then she began.

"I know all of this has happened very quickly for us all," she began. "But I want to make it clear to you that I am not some big city person. I just happened to live in the big city for a time. But that time is over. That part of my life is over. I was never able to adjust to life in Manhattan. It just didn't fit for me. Most of the time, I was miserable. If I didn't have my teaching, and of course, my writing, I don't know how I could have existed. In all the time I lived there I had only one friend, Cousin Ellen. I'll admit that I was not looking forward to coming here, but from the moment I saw you all, something happened to me. I was afraid to admit how perfectly right this all seemed. I could not explain how comfortable it was being here. That was something I never felt in Manhattan. I didn't know it until I got here, but this is what I have been looking for all my life. It was perfect from the start, but just a bit scary. I didn't belong here. Here I was, a short time visitor who quickly realized I did not want to leave. I could not believe three beautiful children like you even existed. I couldn't imagine writing anything better than you three. And Aunt Clara, a person I so wished my own mother could have been, but sadly, never would be. As for Injun Jim, where on earth could you ever find someone like Injun Jim?" Then Martha paused, she did know how this next revelation was going to go over but she promised herself to be honest to a fault, so she had no choice but to plow forward. "And then I saw your father. Oh my. I could not take my eyes off him."

At first there was silence as the children and Aunt Clara nervously shifted in their seats and looked to one another. Giggles began to fill the air followed by full-blown laughter. Aunt Clara just beamed. Martha sensed it was all right to continue.

"I felt like that girl in the fairytale when she saw her Prince Charming for the very first time. I find it so amusing that my writing, my God-given talent, helped me to become a celebrity. That has always fascinated me. It certainly was not something I could have imagined for myself. But now, I am convinced that all that happened so I could be here with you. The sages say there are no accidents. I am now convinced of that. My coming here was no accident. And if you'll have me, this is exactly where I intend to stay."

"Can we call you 'Mommy'?" Thomas wanted to know. For once, Mary did not take exception to his words. It was something she had wanted to ask but, maybe not so soon. Lillith's eyes grew wider, if that were possible. Her only concern was Martha's answer. Aunt Clara had to admit that it was something that definitely needed to be addressed. All waited for Martha's response.

"I'd really like that," she said. "It would be such an honor to have you call me your mom. And I promise, I will do everything I can to honor your Mommy. I just hope there is a place for both of us in your hearts. If it weren't for her, we would not be having this conversation and I would have missed out on so much."

The children jumped up and hugged Martha. Aunt Clara sat back in her chair, a look of total satisfaction spread over her face. Martha had said all she needed to hear. For Aunt Clara, the deal was done.

"Okay, okay," Martha said. "If that's all over, it's time for surprises. There are three boxes in the hallway. Will you children please fetch them and bring them in here? Aunt Clara, would you please call my husband and ask him to join us? We've been apart too long."

"You've got it, Dearie," said Aunt Clara as she left to make the call. The children came running back onto the porch with the boxes. Each had a name attached to it. Once Sam and Injun Jim rejoined them, the children were allowed to open the boxes bearing their name. Squeals of delight could be heard all the way down to the harbor as the children pulled out one fantastic outfit after another. Everything they would possibly need for the trip had been bought, and all with Martha's own money. Aunt Clara just loved the look of pride on her nephew's face. The children held their clothes up to show them off. Martha may have been from the country, but her taste was clearly big city. It was obvious to all, that Martha had made the decision that her children were going to be the best dressed in any crowd.

Later, everybody, including Injun Jim, went up to the Black Swan for dinner. Wanda Loomis held court and all the locals got a chance to mingle with the Tyler clan. Martha could not believe how her life had turned around; more like upside down. And, in so short a time. She had to pinch herself to make sure this was all real. Then she noticed something pressing up against her side. It was Lillith. It was obvious that, from now on, she and Lilith would be joined at the hip.

CHAPTER FOUR

Martha helped Aunt Clara clear the breakfast dishes away. Aunt Clara washed and Martha dried.

"The girls and I need to get a few personal items from the pharmacy down in Old Saybrook. Would you ask Injun Jim to please take us?" she asked.

"Consider it done. When do you want to go?" asked Aunt Clara.

"Give us five minutes," answered Martha.

Injun Jim brought the car up to the back porch and waited for his passengers. Soon they were headed up Pratt Street towards Old Saybrook.

"Oh darn," said Martha. "I forgot something. Take us back! I know right where it is. It will only take a minute."

Injun Jim turned left on N. Main St. and then left again heading back down Main Street towards the house.

"There are Heather and Mrs. Morrissey!" shouted Mary.

Sure enough, Heather Morrissey and her mother were walking down Main Street in front of the Black Swan.

"Stop the car!" Martha demanded. Injun Jim obliged, but was a little apprehensive. He didn't know Martha all that well, so he had no idea what to expect. His instincts told him there was trouble brewing.

"Everyone, stay in the car," she ordered. "I'll be right back." With that, Martha exited the vehicle and stood in the path blocking the Morrissey ladies.

"Oh boy," Injun Jim groaned. Things weren't looking so good. Mary rolled her window down. She and her siblings were anxious to hear every word. Injun Jim did the same.

"I'd like a word with you, Mrs. Morrissey. I understand you have some very strong opinions where I am concerned."

Millicent Morrissey and Martha stood about the same height, but that was the only similarity they shared. Millicent was frumpy and looked older than her years. It was obvious she placed much more emphasis on being a busybody then on one that was well kept.

"I have no idea who you are or what you are talking about," she said.

"Allow me to introduce myself. I am Martha Tyler, and you seem to take a great interest in my affairs. Your daughter informed my daughter concerning me and my family."

"My daughter is mistaken. I don't know what you are talking about," said Millicent.

"Mother," cried Heather, "how could you?"

"Be quiet, Heather," Millicent said. "Don't you dare contradict me, young lady."

Heather did as her mother ordered. She quietly stood there with a face full of hurt and shame. By now a small gathering of townsfolk were standing close by. No one knew what to expect. Martha just stood there, staring into Millicent's eyes. Then she took a menacing step forward. A look of horror came over Millicent's face as she awkwardly took one step back, nearly stumbling and falling. Once again, everyone was waiting to see what Martha would do next. Martha placed her hands on her hips and allowed a broad smile to form on her face.

"That's what I thought," she said, mostly for her own satisfaction. I'm fully aware of people like you. You have a lot to say when people are not around to defend themselves." With a look of contempt, she turned and got back into the car.

"Let's go," she said.

Injun Jim smiled and placed the car in gear and put his foot down on the accelerator. Millicent was left standing there humiliated with many of the townsfolk as witnesses. She grabbed Heather in hand and headed back up Main Street, disgraced by this outsider. Many of the men who witnessed the confrontation expressed glee that someone finally gave Millicent her due. Of course, the story would grow with each telling. This new Mrs. Tyler sure was a firebrand. She gained a lot of new friends this day, and of course, one enemy.

Mary hadn't said a word, but she could not stop smiling. "Martha Tyler," "my daughter;" those were the words she heard Martha use. At that very moment, the second female Tyler child became Martha's. Mary could not wait to tell Aunt Clara. It would soon be apparent to everyone that when the Tylers needed to circle their wagons, Martha would be right there, driving the lead wagon.

CHAPTER FIVE

At 5:45 PM, the train from New York City rolled slowly into Washington DC's magnificent Union Station. If the children were in awe of Grand Central station in Manhattan, they were about to have their child-sized socks knocked off by the grandeur of one of the grandest structures in our nation's capital; the beaux arts magnificence of designer David Birmingham, creator of this amazing structure at the turn of the twentieth century.

The Tyler clan enlisted the services of a porter to deal with their luggage, and then made their way to the Grand Concourse. The eyes of Thomas and Lilith were instantly transfixed on the monumental 96-foot "barrel vaulted" ceiling brushed with 22 karat gold paint. But it was Mary who grabbed onto Martha and whispered, "Oh, Mommy, this is so beautiful." Indeed, "beautiful" hardly described the world's largest train station covering a whopping 200 acres with 75 miles of tracking, and built at a staggering price of $125 million, in 1907. Martha was the first to notice three young men, all dressed in dark suits, hurriedly making their way towards them.

"Captain Tyler, Captain Tyler," called the one in the lead.

"I am Captain Tyler, young man. What can I do for you?" Sam asked.

"I am Jimmy Cummings, Sir, special assistant to Congressman Hayes and these two young men are the Congressman's pages. We are here to escort you to the Willard. We have a limo waiting to take you and your family there."

"Do you have some form of identification?" said Sam.

The lead man showed Sam his credentials. In all honesty, the three standing there looked too young and nervous to pose any threat. Without prompting, the assistant informed Sam, "The Congressman was notified of your arrival by someone of influence, in Essex. Once Congressman Hayes informed the President that you were coming here, the President himself insisted we meet you and extended his personal greetings to you and your family. I can explain on the way, Sir. Congressman Hayes is waiting for us at the Willard."

Sam didn't have to think very hard to guess that none other than Arlen Templeton was responsible for orchestrating all this. Martha let Sam know that she had come to the same conclusion. It was pure Arlen all the way. The man had style.

Congressman Robert Hayes greeted Sam and the family as they entered the halls of Washington's most magnificent and luxurious hotel. The jaw-dropping elegance of the Willard was almost too much for the Tyler children to take in. Martha knew they had never seen anything like this; and that Washington would be like some mystical magical kingdom for them. But it was her desire to expose the children to the one place where they could experience the spirit of our nation. She wanted them to absorb, if that were possible, a place that truly exemplified what America stood for—all America, not just their little corner of the world in Essex, Connecticut. Someday, they would go out into the world. Much would be expected of them, considering their lineage. There was no better place to start their education than the city that bears the name of our first great president, George Washington.

The Willard, known as the crown jewel of Pennsylvania Avenue, is located a mere stone's throw from the White House, the Capitol Building and the National Mall with its unmistakable centerpiece, the Washington Monument.

Recognizing the congressman posed no problem for Martha or Sam. Indeed, he looked like an advertisement for what any self-respecting congressman should look like, and of course wear. His appearance was average in height and weight, with hair parted slightly to the left and tightly combed. His dark brown suit was obviously not tailored, shouting "off the rack" for sure. He was sporting a hopelessly unstylish yellow tie, compliments of last year's collection, with brown stripes tied in the obligatory Windsor knot. This was not a very attractive man. Congressman-looking, of course, but definitely, not attractive. He welcomed the Tylers with the official politician's painted smile. Martha was sure there was a school that taught such things.

Sam knew how to play the game. He responded to the congressman's salutations with some of his own. Martha on the other hand had to shake herself out of her disbelief, but managed to pull it off.

"So good to see you, Captain Tyler. And what a lovely family you have. It is my honor to welcome you to our nation's capital. Please forgive this intrusion but the President, himself, was most adamant that a hero such as yourself should receive our warmest welcome." Before Sam could respond, the Congressman charged ahead. "We have taken the liberty to upgrade your accommodations. I have secured the Washington suite for your family, as it has everything, I believe, you will need to make your stay satisfying and comfortable."

Sam had reserved two adjoining rooms. He and Martha were sure that would be sufficient. Obviously, the congressman or the president or whoever, felt differently.

"We have received a communiqué from someone who has my ear, and amazingly, that of the president; someone who is very close to you and your children. He assured us that you would find our efforts to assist you in your stay acceptable. Now, if it's alright with you, Sir, the hotel staff will see to it that you get settled in and have a chance to freshen up. I have made reservations for you at eight this evening in the hotel's wonderful award-winning restaurant. Jimmy will be at your disposal during your stay to help you with any arrangements you deem necessary and, by the way, I chose the Washington suite because it has a dining room table that accommodates ten with a prep kitchen to make your first day here less hectic. Breakfast will be served in your suite at anytime you choose. Just tell Jimmy what time is convenient and he will make all the arrangements," said the congressman.

"Then I believe it only proper that Jimmy have breakfast with us. Nine o'clock should be about right," said Martha.

The look on Jimmy Cumming's face was priceless. He was caught completely off guard by such a gracious gesture, a totally out-of-character offering, considering his place as a server. He looked to the congressman for assurance. Once again, that politician's smile came forth as Hayes gave his approval. What was behind that smile was anybody's guess.

Sam looked over at Martha with a smile of his own; this one, of warm approval, and just a little bit of wonderment. "What a lovely gesture," he thought to himself. This new Mrs. Tyler seemed capable of one surprise after another. For a brief moment there was an awkward silence.

"Well," the congressman broke in, "if you are ready, Jimmy will see that you get settled in. Remember, he is at your disposal." He made his exit announcing that he had an important meeting demanding his presence.

"Of course you do," thought Martha to herself. She was quickly getting the hang of this Washington two-step. Born and raised in New England, Martha had a real problem with pomposity and pleasantness that was merely an act. New York wasn't New England but it sure was real. No one had any time to play games and that was just the way she liked it. It was Martha who took Jimmy in charge, and after getting Sam and the children settled in, sat down with him to find the best way for them to work together. It had been quite some time since Jimmy had contact with someone who appeared so real. Washington is a power center, and most of the people Jimmy came in contact with were only too willing to play the power game and display some of their own. Martha seemed to understand this, almost immediately, and wanted to lay some ground rules.

"My children are from my husband's first wife who is deceased. I have only come into their lives quite recently. It is absolutely critical to me that they enjoy every moment of their stay here. Neither I nor my husband has any need for pomp and circumstance but, make no mistake, he is a very strong man and a loving father. As far as Samuel is concerned, he merely served his country; he did his job, one that he gets paid to do. As you can see, he does it very well. But, I, and she emphasized the I, am very concerned that he and the children enjoy themselves. Whatever you need to discuss, you can do it with me. I have my husband's complete approval. I sense that is going to be strange or even somewhat difficult for you. But, if you are going to spend time with the Tylers, then you will spend it as a friend of the Tylers and certainly not as a servant. If you can deal with that, I'm sure we are all going to have a great time."

Martha stood up, a sign that the meeting was over. Jimmy scrambled to his feet, still reeling at the words of this Tyler woman. They shook hands and Jimmy made his exit. It wasn't til later, while sharing dinner with his girlfriend that he realized that Mrs. Tyler was none other than Martha Frost, the writer of the day and his girlfriend's favorite. Jimmy had to wipe his brow at that little bit of information. He had known Martha for less than an hour and he already liked her, immensely. Of course, he spent the rest of the evening answering the myriad of questions his girlfriend asked about Martha Frost. Questions like "What was she wearing? What color was her hair and how did she wear it? Did you get a look at her purse, her shoes? How did she act; was she nice?"

Jimmy realized that this visit was probably going to wear him out. He went back to his apartment, got everything ready for the next day and went to bed earlier than he could remember in some time. But, he did have a smile on his face.

CHAPTER SIX

The sound of bells was going off in Sam's head. Finally, he realized it was the telephone next to his bed. He glanced over at the clock to see that it was 7 a.m. Reluctantly, he grabbed for the receiver.

"Concierge calling, Sir," came the pleasant voice on the other end.

"How can anyone be so cheerful this early?" Sam wanted to know.

"The kitchen staff would like to know what time you and your family will be requiring breakfast so that we can prepare it for you."

Sam rolled over and looked at Martha who was now barely awake and looking at him with that "Who is it?" look.

"It's for you," he said dryly, as he handed the receiver to her.

Martha's half-believing look said, "What?" Finally, she took the receiver and attempted a halfway intelligent conversation with the concierge.

"Give us an hour and a half," she managed to get out, "and please contact Jimmy Cummings, Congressman Hayes's special assistant. I am sure the front desk has his number if you don't." She then handed the receiver back to Sam.

"I am going to shower first, then put on my face and get the clothes out for the children," she informed her husband. "Then, you can shower while I get the children up. That shouldn't take me more than forty minutes."

Sam turned over and fluffed his pillow. "Sounds good to me," he said, and nothing else.

Martha just stared at the back of his head, then grudgingly, got out of bed and headed for the shower. She never saw the smile of total satisfaction on Sam's face.

❋　❋　❋

"Okay kids," came Martha's greeting as she entered the children's room. "Time to rise and shine. We've got a little more than half an hour before breakfast. Everybody up, wash your face, and put the clothes on that I have laid out for you. Pancakes, eggs and bacon for everyone," she proclaimed in a voice filled with excitement.

The girls jumped out of bed and ran to the bathroom. Thomas was taking a more deliberate approach. Before long, the girls came out full of energy, talking a blue streak. They could not wait to put on the clothes that Martha had carefully prepared for them.

"Thomas," said Martha, "you go into the bathroom and wash up and take these clothes and get dressed in there. Call out when you are done."

Thomas got slowly to his feet. He collected his clothes and dragged himself into the bathroom. Mary was about to make a comment but was prevented from doing so by a glaring Lilith who stood in the path between her two siblings. She may have been the youngest, but showed no fear of standing up to her older sister. Mary simply backed down and began getting dressed. Of course, she could not resist muttering to herself.

Luckily for her, she was the only one who knew what she was saying. Lilith had her suspicions, but was too busy putting on her new clothes and looking at herself in the mirror. She was very pleased by the vision staring back at her.

The kitchen staff arrived at 8:15, allowing themselves 15 minutes to set the table, set up the prep kitchen and serve. Jimmy came shortly after, and at 8:30 the Tyler clan and Jimmy sat down to a sumptuous breakfast served on the Washington Suite's special china, reserved for royalty, heads of state and honored guests.

Sam and the children engaged in animated conversation while Martha and Jimmy discussed the day's itinerary. Martha was relieved to hear that Jimmy had actually prepared a two-day itinerary that included the ride back to Union Station to meet the train to Charleston, South Carolina. Today's schedule included the Capitol, the Lincoln Memorial, a fun-filled lunch at the Mayflower, then a trip to Mount Vernon, the home of George Washington. Dinner would take place at the famous Martin's Tavern in Georgetown.

Tomorrow, they would visit the Library of Congress, take a walk through Arlington National Cemetery, once the home of Robert E. Lee and finally, visit the White House. The President was away, clearing the way for an honored visitor and his family to make a leisurely visit.

When breakfast was finished, the family washed up and at Martha's insistence, made a final bathroom run for the kids. They then made their way down to the lobby where Jimmy was waiting to escort them.

"This came for you Captain, just a few minutes ago," said Jimmy Cummings. "A courier brought it to the front desk and they gave it to me, knowing I was waiting for you. The man simply delivered it to the desk, refusing to bring it up to your room. He said his instructions were to do that and nothing more."

Sam took the envelope and opened it. The message was simple. It was a man's name written in script. Adam Weishaupt was the name staring back at him. Sam looked confused and showed it to Martha. They agreed that the name was somewhat familiar, but neither could connect it.

"Give me a minute," said Sam as he made his way over to the hotel telephones. After a few moments he came back. Then he and the family followed Jimmy through the magnificent Peacock Alley which links the lobby to the main entrance. Peacock Alley is a Washington must-see, all in itself. Two lines of magnificent marble columns rise to 25 feet high ceilings, each with a huge accompanying decorative planter, while chandeliers and sconces provide brilliant illumination from high above. This gigantic room gives a whole new perspective to what is commonly known as the "watering hole." Certainly, one could relax and partake of liquid comfort, but make no mistake, this is the place to see and to be seen. It has become a Washington tradition, actually a must. Anyone who is anyone, and that includes presidents, traverse this hallowed grand hallway. Then, tea at the Peacock is the reason tourists come from all over to experience this enclave of sheer elegance and afternoon refreshment.

"I know that name. I just can't place it. I called Aunt Clara and told her to get in touch with Injun Jim. Believe it or not, if anyone would know the name it would be him. And if he doesn't, believe me, he will find out. That's one of his favorite things to do. The man loves to study history and the biographies of famous people," Sam told Martha. "Maybe if we know who he is, we can figure out why he is contacting me here. In any event,

Aunt Clara will get in touch with Injun Jim and get him on it. It will probably make his day.

Martha simply smiled at the news. It seemed as though every day brought a new discovery in her new life as a Tyler.

No sooner had the family gotten back to their suite after their first day's foray into Washington DC, Sam took notice of the blinking light on the telephone. He went over, picked up the receiver, and dialed the front desk.

"You have a call from Clara Tyler," Sam was informed. Sam immediately called Aunt Clara while Martha took charge of the children to get them washed up and put on a change of clothes for dinner in Georgetown, at the famous Martin's Tavern. Of course, Martin's had hamburgers and legendary french fries for the children. Their dessert menu was really something. This evening would be all about them.

"Injun Jim has been coming out of his skin since I called him. The poor man is so excited I almost had to put cold compresses on him to calm him down," said Aunt Clara.

"Is he there now?" Sam asked.

"Hasn't left, not even for a minute. Must be something real important to set him off like that," said Aunt Clara. She then yelled to Injun Jim who was nervously pacing back and forth on the porch. He charged through the screen door and hastily grabbed the phone from Clara's hand.

"Do you have any idea who this man is?" asked Injun Jim.

"And it's real nice to hear your voice, too," said Sam.

"What, oh, sorry about that, Captain. I don't know what's going on down there, but you seem to find secret societies wherever you go. I guess the Skull and Bones were not enough for you. Now you've come up with something that may have had a great impact on that there Yale group."

"And that would be?" Sam asked.

"Hold on to your hat; none other than the Illuminati," said Injun Jim with barely controlled excitement.

Sam grew silent. The Illuminati, a group originating in Bavaria, was one of the most secretive groups ever. Their brief history took place in the middle to late 1700s. They believed in a society neither governed by government nor the church. They reasoned that intelligence and reason were the keys to a Utopian society. Of course, Weishaupt and his followers believed that they were the ones who possessed the intelligence and reason to run such a Utopian society. They were not above overthrowing the existing powers by whatever means necessary. Their proximity to and influence over Germany was not lost on Sam. Linking their beliefs to the insanity of the Nazis did not require much of a stretch. Still, Sam had to wonder why someone would send this message to him. And why here, why now? Sam sat down on the bed. This revelation made absolutely no sense to him. And besides, who could possibly know he was here in Washington? That question bothered him the most.

"You still there?" Injun Jim wanted to know.

"Yes, Jim. Sorry," said Sam. "Please go ahead. Is there more?"

"You betcha," said Injun Jim. "These fellers played for keeps. Word is, they no longer exist, but don't you believe it. Somehow, they are connected to the Templars, the Masons and even the Skulls. You see, those organizations are all about secrecy. Some folks believe the Illuminati still exists. They are convinced they just went underground and infiltrated these organizations. That makes more sense than buying into their disappearance. They also bring something new to these groups—paranoia. It's that "us against the world" way of looking at things that makes them so darn dangerous. Believe me, they don't trust nobody. There is even some rumblings now about a new secret order in the Catholic Church, thanks to them. This thing can get pretty scary."

Sam waited till the children had been tucked into bed before revealing all this news to Martha. The family had spent one wonderful day in the capital and this evening found one very tired bunch. Martha joined Sam for a glass of wine in the living room. He told her all that Injun Jim had revealed. Martha's reaction to the news was pretty much the same as Sam's. She just sat there silently and sipped her wine. But the wheels inside her head were turning.

"Let's keep a tight rein on the children tomorrow," said Sam.

"Yes, I was thinking the same thing. But we don't want to get too paranoid ourselves and make the children nervous. That would ruin everything," said Martha.

"Exactly," said Sam. "This might be nothing, but, then again . . . ." his words trailed off. But Martha already knew what he was thinking. The coming together of their minds was beginning to be apparent to both of them. It was as though their minds have been waiting for each other. Sam could not believe how close he and Martha had grown in such an amazingly short amount of time.

"I told Injun Jim to poke around, discreetly," he said, "and see if anyone back in Essex talked about our plans. Sam was beginning to regret being so open about the trip. He was also feeling a little sad that from now on, he and Martha would have to be very careful who knew about them. It was too soon to know what all this meant, but one thing was for sure, someone did know their plans and that someone was sending a message. Just what that message was wasn't clear yet. But again, if paranoia was their goal, then they were now at least partially successful.

Jimmy Cummings had contributed mightily to the wonderful visit for the children. Martha explained to him what was going on, and Jimmy stepped right up to allow Sam and her to be more aware of their surroundings, and sadly, everyone around them. As they boarded the train at Union Station, Martha gave Jimmy an extra strong embrace. He was taken aback by such a display of affection and gratitude from someone he hardly knew.

"Sam and I can never thank you enough," she said. "If you are ever in our neck of the woods, please come and see us. The Tylers owe you a debt of gratitude. And I will not forget how you helped me give my family such a wonderful experience."

As the train began to pick up steam, and make its way along the tracks exiting the station, Jimmy just stood there, savoring the memory of his encounter with the Tylers. The children took to him instantly, and though delighted to be on their way to another adventure, expressed sadness to have to leave their newfound friend behind. Jimmy Cummings would not soon forget a rare two days he had just spent in Washington DC. He did not know it at the time, but he had formed a bond with the Tylers of Wolf Harbor.

"Glad that's behind us," said Sam, as he and Martha relaxed in their compartment. The children were in the adjoining one resting before dinner.

"I think we can breathe a little easier now that that's over," said Martha. "It will be a welcome relief to be in the relaxed atmosphere of South

Carolina. I'm sure we will all feel safer the farther we get away from the fast-paced Northeast.

Sam nodded in agreement. But Sam was a cop. And this was his family. He was not so sure about all that Martha said. The South sure appeared friendly, but Sam knew crime was the same everywhere, even if it came with a smile on its face. Sam's guard would not soon be let down. He sat back, closed his eyes and took a deep breath. He could not stop thinking that out of nowhere, he gets a letter bearing simply the name of one of the world's most infamous people, the man who created the Illuminati. Was South Carolina really going to be safer? That little message bearing only Adam Weishaupt's name changed everything.

CHAPTER SEVEN

One Week Later:

Martha made her way across the lawn connecting her and Sam's home to that of Aunt Clara. Her morning shower had little effect on waking her up. The children were still in bed enjoying the last few mornings of their vacation. They could sleep in and not have to get up early for school. With eyes barely open, Martha noticed Sam's car in Aunt Clara's driveway. This surprised her. Even though Sam had nearly a week left to his vacation he had told her he was going down to the barracks in Clinton, to check on things and see how everything was going. Martha found Sam and Aunt Clara sitting at the kitchen table when she made her way up the stairs and through the screen door. Each had a cup of coffee in front of them that they had hardly touched. There were solemn looks on both of their faces.

"Something is wrong," Martha said. She waited for a reaction.

"Sam's been trying to reach Cousin Caroline since yesterday," said Aunt Clara. "She never came home from the date she went on a few nights ago."

"That would be the day we left for home," said Martha.

"Right," said Sam, "and no one has seen or heard from her since. The man she was with has not been seen either. I called FBI Headquarters and spoke to her supervisor. She has not seen Caroline. She told me that her absence was unusual. Caroline is one of her best people. She had the highest rating in her sector. I'm starting to get a bad feeling about this."

Martha poured herself a cup of coffee, a habit she had recently acquired since becoming a Tyler. "What can we do?" she asked Sam.

"I've spoken to the police chief down in Columbia. He seems to be a good man. They are stretched pretty thin down there. Many of his people are serving in the war. Remember, Columbia is the state capital. He has serious responsibilities and a depleted force. Some old-timers have been trying to help out, but there is concern for their safety."

Just then, the telephone rang. It was Malcolm White, the police chief in Columbia. Sam thanked him by name for calling over at Aunt Clara's. He had called over at the house and Mary gave him this number. Neither Tyler woman liked the expression on Sam's face as he listened to the words offered by the voice on the other end. Sam's body language signaled that the news definitely was not making him very happy. After a few moments, Sam thanked the chief and came back to the table. He slowly took his seat and stared down at the table.

"Okay, Sam," said Aunt Clara, "what's going on?"

"Nothing is confirmed yet," said Sam, "but there was a double homicide in Sumter. They found a car with two dead bodies near the lake over at Poinsett State Park. There are a lot of walking trails over there. A couple of hikers discovered the car. Both bodies inside were burned beyond recognition; the car was completely destroyed by fire."

Martha and Aunt Clara reacted with shock.

"Considering the nature of the crime, the chief has sent the remains to the FBI lab," Sam continued. His voice was starting to become emotional.

"They are not even sure of the make or model of the automobile, but managed to get the serial number. It will take at least 24 hours before they know anything. My feeling is it doesn't look good. I'm sorry, Aunt Clara. Caroline is Uncle William's only child. I hope I'm wrong but my senses tell me that I am not. The chief did say that the young man she was seeing was fairly new to the area; he also said something about him just didn't add up. A check on his name came up empty. His Social Security number and identifications are all forgeries. Caroline's involvement with this man is beginning to come into question. Her desk and home are being searched by the Bureau to she if was involved in anything. I can't believe this is happening. We were just there. There was not even a hint of anything out of the ordinary in Caroline's demeanor. If one of the bodies is hers, I will be flying down there. Is that okay with you, Martha?" said Sam.

"Of course," was Martha's immediate response. Then she thought for a moment and said, "I do have to get the children ready for school. Labor Day is only eight days away. We'll busy ourselves with that. But, you won't be gone all week will you?"

"No," said Sam. "I just want to get down there and make some contacts so I can keep up with the investigation. I'll put in a call to Matt D'Onofrio. He might know someone at the New York Bureau office who could possibly pave the way. But let's not get ahead of ourselves. I'll get all my things ready. Let's hope I won't need to go," said Sam.

Martha could not believe that a wonderful vacation could end in such tragedy. Sam and Caroline had not had much contact since she went off to college. She took a job at the FBI to get knowledge of the crime-fighting aspect of the American justice system. On top of that, she had a position as legal assistant to a federal judge awaiting her. It seemed inconceivable that Caroline could be part of any wrongdoing.

❋   ❋   ❋

Martha found herself sitting alone at Aunt Clara's kitchen table. She got up and emptied her half—cold coffee which she never drank and poured herself a fresh cup. Sam went back home to make some calls while Aunt Clara excused herself to make up her bed and attend to some laundry. She leaned against the kitchen sink and allowed her mind to drift back to their time in Columbia. Martha could not have hoped for better results on her first trip with the family. Columbia was all she had hoped for and more. Tree-lined streets with beautifully preserved stately homes dating back before the Civil War. These and even some going all the way back to the Revolutionary War were everywhere. Fort Sumter was one of the many historic sites, although its significance was not lost on the children, especially Thomas. Thomas wanted to know everything about all things historical. More than once he nearly drove the family insane with his constant questions. Mary was more interested in romance and the romantic novelists of the area. It was here that she discovered Julia Dietermayorkin whose story, "Scarlet Sister Mary," won the Pulitzer Prize in 1920.

"For goodness sake," exclaimed her father, "she's not even a teenager yet! Is this normal behavior?" he wanted to know.

Martha just lowered her head to avoid showing him the broad all-knowing smile spread across her face. "The poor man has no idea what lies in store for him," she thought to herself.

Lilith, on the other hand, was all wonderment. Everything fascinated her. Such beauty, such charm, the homes, the gardens, the restaurants, the genteel way of life. To her, Columbia had the same small town feel as Essex, but it was so much more elegant. For Lilith, it was all magical; the giant hanging moss, the stately, timeless oak trees, the way people dressed and seemed to embrace life. How Lilith wished she could take this wonderful place back home to Essex. But most of all, Lillith's greatest source of joy was that Martha and her daddy were here, spending this time with her, Thomas and Mary. She would not stop telling Martha it was the best time of her life. And, now, tragedy had struck to steal away some of the magic. Martha was determined to preserve as much of it as possible while keeping a proper respect for the Tyler family's grief.

CHAPTER EIGHT

Police Chief White met Sam at the airport. It was a somber ride to police headquarters. The female body had been identified as Caroline Tyler. The chief had the unenviable task of telling Sam the grisly tale of his cousin's murder.

"We found some articles believed to belong to the victims near the Lake. I believe they were intended to look like a robbery and the discarding of things of no value to the killer or killers. But I don't believe that is the case," said the chief. Sam took in what the chief told him. He didn't want to interrupt. It was important not to break the chief's train of thought. He motioned for the chief to go on.

"I spoke with some of the boys at the FBI and they were kind enough to share some information with me. First of all, let me say, and I mean no disrespect, Sam, they are not too interested in finding out who killed your cousin. What keeps them in the game at all is the fact that the male victim, known to us as Louis Martin, is really Martin Kempler, a German nationalist in this country illegally. From what we can piece together, he was probably trying to get close to your cousin, but it doesn't appear that he had nearly enough time for that. He's only been here a couple of weeks. By the way, the plates on his vehicle were stolen. The auto is the property of Martin Kempler. We're just about one hundred percent sure he was the male victim. Now here's the really interesting part. Until he came down here, Kempler lived in your backyard. He lived in a boarding house in Milford, Connecticut. How's that for the long arm of coincidence?"

Sam was taken completely by surprise. There was, however, one thing in his favor. Milford was in his jurisdiction and close to New Haven. At least he could take an active role in the investigation. It was a card he would hold onto to play in the game that included the FBI. Having things close to home would seem to be playing in his favor. His reverie was quickly broken.

"I have to tell you this, Sam, and believe me it won't be easy," said Chief White. "Whoever did this thing was real mad at somebody. The arms and legs of both victims were broken. That means they were probably alive when the vehicle was torched. That was a pretty sadistic thing to do. Takes a real cold-blooded individual to do such a thing. Those two people really suffered, Sam, but I gotta level with you. Don't get your hopes up that this crime is going to get solved anytime soon or ever. We just don't have the manpower or the finances to have much hope. The FBI will definitely hold out information from us and drop us just as soon as they can. Hoover's boys are all take and no give. I'll do my best to find out as much as I can and see you get everything I have. I'm real sorry, Sam. Folks around here really liked Caroline. Her colleagues at the Bureau thought she was real special. I'm just sorry we can't do more."

Sam really liked the chief. He was a good man who appeared to be a good police officer; one with a heart. Sam went over to the historic Rose Hall Bed and Breakfast and checked in. He booked two nights. Along with its many charms the Rose Hall was located near the lovely University of South Carolina campus, and just a few blocks off Gervais Street, the main thoroughfare linking all of Columbia. As he rode along the beautiful tree-lined wide boulevard that was Gervais Street, he found he could easily understand why Caroline chose to live in such a place. The amazing thing about Columbia was that it actually benefited from Sherman's march to the sea, during the Civil War. Because Savanna was surrounded by swamplands, Sherman chose to avoid torching it, choosing instead to go through Columbia on his march towards Atlanta. Because of the devastating cruelty of Sherman's troops, Columbia had to be reconstructed. Thankfully, the founding fathers improved upon what was already there. The openness of the boulevard and streets was definitely not characteristic of all other historic towns of the South; it was definitely unique.

Sam reasoned a two-night stay would be quite enough to accomplish all that he had set out to do. He was a veteran police officer and knew these things take time. Staying any longer would accomplish very little and might create some unnecessary tension for Chief White. Sam wanted to get back home, but needed to see to Caroline's remains. Aunt Clara told him to make arrangements to have her remains sent back to Essex, so that she could be buried with her mother and father. Aunt Clara would take care of the arrangements.

Sam had a 10 AM meeting with Special Agent Warren Romney of the FBI. Romney was not a very congenial sort. He was not too keen on sharing information outside of the Bureau. He was a real hardliner who succeeded in getting Sam to the point where he wanted to invite the man outside so he could box him around the parking lot. But taking into consideration the fact that they were both officers of the law he decided to forgo the pleasure. In any event, Sam realized that Chief White could get whatever he needed to know out of Romney and then pass it along to him. He was happy to take his leave of the FBI and Romney in particular. Now he was anxious to get back home so he could start piecing together everything he had concerning Martin Kempler, also known as Louis Martin. During his visit Sam made another discovery. He absolutely hated sleeping in a bed that did not have Martha in it.

CHAPTER NINE

Sam stood waiting patiently as one piece of luggage after another rolled past him on the huge conveyor belt, at Fiorello LaGuardia Airport in Queens, N.Y. Finally, he recognized his suitcase approaching and reached down to retrieve it. He then headed towards the terminal exit. After a brief wait, he secured a taxi to take into Manhattan and Grand Central Station. The flight had been smooth, but it had little effect calming down Sam's emotions which were jockying back and forth somewhere between anger and disbelief.

Caroline Tyler was one of the sweetest, nicest human beings Sam had ever known. From her earliest childhood she was liked by everyone she knew. She was a Tyler through and through. She worked harder than anyone else, even when she could have taken things easy. She was always tops in her class. The future shined brightly for her. She had everything it took to be a success. And now she was gone; murdered in a most horrible manner.

Sam was a seasoned law officer. He had learned to stay detached from the victims; to look at things objectively, clinically, to bring criminals to justice. But this was his very own cousin who was killed, and with a man nobody seemed to know very much about. On top of that, what little they did know turned out to be false. What was Caroline doing with this person? The obvious answer to Sam was that he must have played on her trusting nature and intended to use her. But, for what? Obviously, he was not around long enough to realize that Caroline was not in a position to help him even though she worked at the Bureau. Or, maybe he did and just didn't care. Caroline had a strange effect on people. They seemed to be drawn to her like a magnet.

Once again, Sam found himself with a myriad of questions and not one single answer. Then again, his reasoning could be all wrong. He was letting his imagination and emotions run rampant and he knew that was not good. He took solace in the fact that he could rely on his good friend Matt D'Onofrio with the New Haven Police Department to help get some answers. Chief White down in Columbia seemed honest enough, and for now, Sam would take him at his word to keep Sam informed if anything useful came up. Then Sam's thoughts drifted uncomfortably towards Warren Romney at the FBI. How sweet it would be, he thought, to land a right cross squarely on that pompous bureaucrat's weak jaw. How many times had he heard Reverend Foster at Saint Peter's preach to the congregation about loving your enemy and forgiving those who come against you. Sam had to admit that this was a difficult concept to embrace where Romney was concerned. "Bless those who curse you," Sam said to himself. "I'd love to bless him, all right; right on the kisser."

Mercifully, Sam's thoughts drifted back to Martha and how much he missed her and the family. The events of the last few days validated his decision to marry Martha as soon as possible. His profession made him constantly aware of how bad things can happen to good people, and how quickly joy can be turned to sorrow. Caroline's death was a devastating loss to the family. Aunt Clara would take it harder than anyone. Knowing how hard this was going to be on her just fueled his angry fire.

Caroline's father, Aunt Clara's brother, was an officer in the Navy, who died on the Arizona at Pearl Harbor. His death sent Caroline's mother over the edge. She spent a short stay in a sanitarium before passing away from a broken heart. The Tylers were no strangers to tragedy, but Caroline was so young, so full of life. For all his experience, Sam was having a difficult time dealing with this.

Sam sensed the train slowing down. Somewhere after New Haven, he must have dozed off. He had not slept very well for days. He grabbed his suitcase and exited the train at Old Saybrook station. Injun Jim was waiting to take him home. Martha had decided to wait with the family. Everyone was anxious for his return, and Martha sensed it would be helpful to Aunt Clara and the children for her to be with them. She was right. Injun Jim immediately sensed that Sam's thoughts were miles away and quickly ceased any attempts at conversation. They were headed down Main Street in Essex, when Sam ordered him to stop the car. They were in front of Saint Peter's Episcopal Church.

"You go home and tell Martha and the family I will be home shortly. I'm going into the church. Please tell Martha not to worry. I won't be long."

Sam walked across the street, climbed the stairs and entered St. Peter's. Injun Jim did as he was told. A look of confusion was on everyone's face as Jim pulled his car into Aunt Clara's driveway.

Before anyone could ask, Jim informed them, "Sam's okay. He just had me drop him off up Main Street at St. Peter's. He told me to tell you he'll be along shortly."

Martha calmed everyone down and told them to wait right there. She would go see to Sam and bring him right home. The disappointed group took seats on the steps leading up to the porch.

Martha went through the large doors leading to the sanctuary and noticed one lone person up front. She quietly made her way up and slid in next to Sam. She could see that he was upset. He took her hand and pulled her close. Neither spoke for a few moments.

"Come on, let's go home," he said, finally.

As they walked down Main Street, Sam told Martha what little he had learned in Columbia, and how much he missed her and the family.

"This is too close to home," he said. "I'm going to find out who did this and make sure they pay for what they have done. I know in my gut that poor Caroline was murdered at the expense of someone else's crimes. I won't rest until that someone is brought to justice."

"We won't rest," said Martha.

That brought a smile to Sam's face. He drew her even closer as they walked down Main Street, his arm wrapped tightly around her.

CHAPTER TEN

Sam's return home was a joyous occasion for the family. The children were not used to his being away. Since their mother died, Sam had spent every moment he could with them. The time he and Martha spent on their honeymoon was the first time he and the children had been apart. His going back to South Carolina was difficult enough for them, but knowing their cousin had been murdered, and their father was going back to the place where it happened was disconcerting for them. Martha worked overtime to keep them busy and in good spirits. She and Aunt Clara grew even closer during this time. Each new day brought the family closer, and now Sam was back and everyone was relieved.

Sam filled Aunt Clara in on all he had learned concerning Cousin Caroline's death. It wasn't much. Aunt Clara had begun to prepare the arrangements to bring Caroline's remains back to Essex. Reverend Foster took care of all the necessary preparations for a memorial service. There would be no visiting hours or formal funeral. Close friends and family would gather to lay poor Caroline to rest. The Tyler clan of Sam's youth was disappearing. First Sally, now Caroline. Sam gently took hold of Aunt Clara's hand as a tear started to flow down her saddened face.

Wanda Loomis, with Injun Jim's help, brought dinner for the whole family. Fried chicken, mashed potatoes, corn on the cob and a huge fresh garden salad; all Sam's favorites were spread over Aunt Clara's dining room table. Fresh baked apple and rhubarb pies were set in the kitchen for after supper dessert. Wanda placed a gallon of vanilla ice cream in Aunt Clara's freezer. It had been some time since the family had sat down to a meal at Aunt Clara's. Sam said grace and placed heavy emphasis on how blessed they were. Friends and family; Sam was grateful for them both.

❉   ❉   ❉

The town folks really turned out for the Labor Day celebration on the town green. The war was heavy on everyone's mind and any chance to celebrate was welcome, indeed. Sam invited Matt D'Onofrio up from New Haven to join them. Matt had a friend in the Milford Police Department who did some checking for him. Milford is a small town just south of New Haven that is rich in history and known as a very tight-knit community. The cannons of Fort Trumbull fired on British frigates during the Revolution and the head of one of its largest farming families, the Treats, was one of Connecticut's earliest governors. Possessing seventeen and one half miles of waterfront, nearly all its public lands accessible to the locals, Milford was a world within itself. Sam's first reaction was that outsiders were not going to find it easy to gain information against one of their own. Then again, Sam came from a small town and had to believe there were at least one or two gossips lurking in the bushes. His prayer would be that he would locate them and find them amenable to his queries.

Matt learned that two men had been renting rooms from the Peet sisters, Agnes and Mildred, who had a home at the tip of Point Lookout, which had an unobstructed view of Milford Harbor, Long Island Sound and the legendary Charles Island, just off the coast of Myrtle Beach. The Peete family dated back to the earliest settlement in Milford and their property was among the most valuable in the town. Two men of unknown origin had been renting rooms until recently when both mysteriously disappeared. Matt's friend told him he was pretty sure at least one of them fit the description of Louis Martin. Their rent had been paid for months in advance, which made their disappearance seem odd. Matt stressed that Milford was a community where everyone knew everyone else's business. It was a pretty fair bet that this information was solid. Sam decided that visiting the Peet sisters would be his first order of business after checking in at headquarters the next day.

As Sam and Matt joined the family, they saw Mayor Tinsley approaching. He was alone. Sam guessed the mayor's relationship with his mystery woman at the wedding reception hadn't worked out. Allison Tinsley, on the other hand, showed up on the arm of an older man whose clothes and manner suggested wealth. The mayor told Sam that Allison's new man was from Boston and that he indeed was from a very wealthy old moneyed family. The mayor also shared that this new relationship with a much older man caused him some concern. But he had learned long ago, that he had very little, if any, influence on Allison's actions. His only recourse was to grin and bear it.

Mary expressed rather dryly that she actually thought she saw Allison smile, just once, that is; but she was pretty sure it was a smile. Once again Martha just looked at her in disbelief. Martha began to say something but thought better of it and let the matter go. She was convinced that Mary's dry wit was inherited from Aunt Sarah. It took a few seconds for her to compose herself. She tried to remember what she was like at Mary's age. She concluded that neither she nor any of her friends were anything remotely like Mary.

The children would be starting school tomorrow and Sam would begin his quest to look into the mystery behind Martin Kempler and his missing companion. Martha had a few days before her new semester at Albertus Magnus was to begin. She had already begun to fashion her next writing project based on her experiences with Sam and the Skull and Bones murder mystery. One thought kept recurring over and over in her mind. Sam was not in this alone. One way or another she was going to be involved in all of it. Just the thought of that was like a jolt of electricity shooting through her body.

CHAPTER ELEVEN

Sam checked in at the Westbrook Barracks and proceeded down Route #1 to New Haven, to check in with Sergeant Matt D'Onofrio. The Sergeant gave him the name of his friend at the Milford Police Department and Sam took the ride down Route #1 to Milford, about 10 miles south of New Haven. Officer William Perkins told Matt to have Sam meet him at a diner on the Boston Post Road, another name for Route #1, at 11 AM. Sam was there right on time and he and Officer Perkins, a twenty—year veteran of the Milford Police Department, engaged in coffee and in animated conversation. Matt was right when he told Sam that people here knew everyone else's business, and Officer Perkins lived up to that statement in every sense of the word.

The officer was well aware of the two men renting rooms from the Peet sisters: something about them just didn't seem to add up to him. They both seemed to have plenty of money, yet no jobs. They had not done anything wrong so there was no justification for investigating them. The officer became suspicious when he observed their clothes which seemed to suit their lifestyle. Milford was shoreline and beaches and water. The two men never seemed to wear anything that suggested vacationing, or interest in the beaches, each a huge Milford tourist attraction. Many people from Westchester County and Rockland County, in New York, spent their summers in Milford. Cottages and hotels were in great supply, yet these two men never seemed interested. In fact, they just seemed to exist, and appeared and disappeared constantly. The officer was sure he once heard them speaking German to each other when they were not aware that he was in earshot. He remembered how nervous they appeared when they became aware of his presence. But still, they did not break any laws; they didn't appear to bother anyone. They were content to take most of their meals prepared by Agnes and Mildred Peet, who were only too happy to have two men folk around, even if the men were considerably younger. Neither sister had married so there were no children to look after. Cooking for these two boys was a welcome change for them. Most renters had family along, and usually did their own cooking or ate at the many eating establishments in town. Then there was one more thing Officer Perkins shared with Sam.

"Some of the locals swear they've seen flashing lights, like signals, going off on the other side of Charles Island and somewhere near Point Lookout. But nobody can verify any of it," said the officer.

"What significance could there be in all of that? You think there might be a German submarine close to shore?" asked Sam.

"Not a chance," said Perkins. "The Coast Guard runs regular checks for such things through the whole Long Island Sound, and so far, no evidence has been found to lead us to believe that to be true."

"Got any thoughts of your own?" Sam asked.

The officer took a deep breath, pushed back on the padded back to his booth seat and seemed to be trying to decide how to begin. Sam, wisely, said nothing, giving the officer all the room he needed.

"This is only speculation," he began, "but I've been doing police work around here for a long time and I'm convinced their presence has something to do with the excavation work done around Charles Island."

"Tell me about this Charles Island," said Sam.

"Charles Island is one of our most treasured attractions here in Milford. Our history dates back to the American Revolution, but Charles Island is pure magic. You see, it's a pretty sure bet that none other than Captain Kidd passed through here in the latter stages of his career, that is before he was captured by the British. One of the well-known local young women documented a night he spent at her Aunt's home; she wasn't very complimentary where the captain was concerned, but no one questions her claim. Folks are convinced Kidd buried a vast treasure somewhere on the island, Captain," said Perkins, "believed to be worth somewhere in the neighborhood of $100 million."

Sam could not believe that he had never heard this story before. He thought he was aware of all the rich folklore where the coastline in that part of the state was concerned. But $100 million is a sum that would attract a lot of attention, especially from Germany, to aid in financing its war effort.

"I would never have considered these two fellows, if I had not heard them speaking German. I may be reading too much into this, but it's very possible they came here to keep tabs on the excavation that was going on around the island."

"Excavation for what?" Sam asked.

"Now that's a real good question, Captain. The island has an amazing history, much more than just Captain Kidd and his treasure. Back before the turn of the century, the island was the property of the wealthy Pritchard

58   ALAN DEL MONTE

family who turned their home into an exclusive resort hotel. The rich used to sail there all through the summer season. Lots of famous folks visited the island until the hotel mysteriously burned to the ground, forcing the Pritchards to abandon it. After many years and much changing of hands, a Catholic religious order took over the island and built a monastery and retreat. Stories used to run wild about a tunnel system started by the Pritchards, and then improved upon by the Aquinas Dominicans."

"Tunnels for what?" Sam wanted to know.

"Some say it started out as a wine cellar, and then again some think there could have been smuggling activity going on by old man Pritchard who, some believe, upset his partners. Thus, the mysterious fire. Liquor is always a valuable commodity. Of course the police never put any stock in that story. Old man Pritchard was just too fine a gentleman. You come from a small town, Captain. You know how people can get. One thing about Milford, this town loves mysteries and conspiracies. What makes more sense is that old man Pritchard was a pretty smart fellow. By the time he expanded his hotel to 75 rooms, it makes perfect sense that underground tunneling would afford him and his workers easy access to all parts of the property. Think about it, no one would have to go outdoors, no matter what the problem or weather. Now that makes a heck of a lot more sense to me, and the town fathers, I might add.

Much happened after the fire. Sarah Pritchard, his daughter, tried to make a go of it before selling out. The property changed hands on numerous occasions for any number of reasons. One owner rebuilt the property to its exact specifications, but for some reason never reopened. He sold the property to the George A. Miles Fish Oil Company and for a good period of time they ran a lucrative business. Then they hit upon hard times, the First

World War was looming and the economy was suffering and once again, a mysterious fire. People can believe whatever they want, but one thing is for sure, those tunnels do exist. And then there is the land bridge."

Perkins could see a confused look working its way across Sam's face.

"At low tide, there is a land bridge connecting the island to Myrtle Beach. People actually drove horse-drawn delivery carts back and forth while the tide was low. Heck, some folks would drive automobiles out there at the turn of the century. Anyway, nobody would suspect any illegal activity if indeed anything like that was going on. Back then, dealers in alcohol in New Haven and New York, would be most grateful for cheap liquor that bypassed the controlling gangster elements who trafficked in such things. Those gangsters might also take a dim view of anyone cheating them out of their very lucrative revenues."

"But let's get back to the monastery. The monks just left one day. No excuses, no nothing. Just up and left. A real mystery. Now that might have been the end of it, except that there was a story about some Spanish gold coins being discovered in Bavaria where the monks spent some time after they left here, before once again, vanishing. Folks believe they ended up in Rome. But who knows if they took off with much treasure or just a few pieces. Whatever, the fact that the coins were discovered in a hidden area of the monastery in Bavaria makes me pretty suspicious.

For years, no one knew who owned the island after that. Talk was the United Illuminating Company, the large electric people, bought the island as part of a plan by the government to expand our electric power capabilities for the war effort. There was a lot of activity out there until a short time ago when all work came to a halt and the workers all left. No one is sure who owns it now, and no one seems to be making any claim to it, so it would be easy for someone to go out there at night and look for the treasure. Too many people visit the island during the daytime. Of course, if the story about those tunnels is true, then who knows who could be out there, and for what reason."

"Then those flashing light signals would make sense, wouldn't they?" said Sam.

"Exactly," said Perkins.

"I think it's time I met the Peet sisters," said Sam.

"Follow me," said Officer Perkins. "My being there will make it easier for you. I knew their daddy well. Heck, everyone around Milford did."

With that, they got up to leave. Sam paid the bill then went to his cruiser to follow Officer Perkins to Point Lookout. One thing Perkins said really caught his attention: Bavaria. If it were true that the Dominican Order really did go to Bavaria and if they brought proof of a treasure, then it made perfect sense that the Germans would buy into the Captain Kidd treasure story, and would probably do almost anything to get their hands on $100 million worth of booty. Sam's mind was racing. Who knows where this was going? But all of a sudden, it was going there real fast. But how on earth could Caroline be any part of this? Sam was too good a policeman to dismiss the long arm of coincidence. One thing was for sure, some Germans were going to pay dearly for ever meeting Caroline Tyler.

Sam followed Officer Perkins through town and over to Gulf Street, which wound its way along the Milford harbor and through one of its larger beaches, Gulf Beach. He could not help noticing how much of the ride showed access to the water. And then, out of the corner of his eye, he spotted it, Charles Island. The island sat with an air of mystery offshore, an unobstructed centerpiece for the eye from any angle. There was nothing to challenge its presence.

Finally, they turned right at Point Lookout Road and proceeded to the very tip and the Peet residence. Immediately, Sam recognized it as similar to the sea captains' homes in Essex and Saybrook. And sure enough, it had the identifying feature that let Sam know that there definitely was a place from which signals could be sent: the widow's walk.

CHAPTER TWELVE

A bright smile and a warm welcome met Sam and Officer Perkins at the front door. Agatha Peet, a slender woman in her early 60's bade the police officers come into her home. She ushered them onto the sun porch which boasted a magnificent panoramic view of Long Island Sound from the far reaches of Montauk, to Charles Island and beyond. Sam's mind was working overtime.

"I just made some iced tea and we always have lemonade handy," said Agatha. "You boys set a while and I'll be right back."

Sam and Officer Perkins took seats overlooking the water. Sunlight danced over the waves as white sails bobbed up and down heading into and out of Milford Harbor. Sam could not get over the great number of sailboats that seemed to be everywhere. Just then Agatha returned, but Sam noticed the dress she had on was a different color from the one she was wearing just a few moments ago.

"The woman must be a quick change artist," Sam thought to himself.

Just then, another woman identical to the first came in wearing the brightly colored dress Sam remembered. The look on Sam's face was priceless. He looked over at Officer Perkins who could hardly contain his laughter.

"He didn't tell you we were twin sisters, did he?" said Agatha. "The boy has a real wicked sense of humor; always had, even as a youngster.

Sam looked menacingly in Officer Perkins' direction then took hold of the hand being extended to him.

"I am Mildred Peet, Captain Tyler. Welcome to our home. It's a real shame you had to experience William's shenanigans. Folks around here are kind of used to his antics," said Agatha's sister.

Sam could see the playful attitude Mildred had towards the officer. He also noticed that her sister was not in such a playful mood. She muttered something under her breath with a face that showed that Officer Perkins was not one of her favorites. It didn't take Sam long to discover that she was the more serious and maternal of the twin sisters.

"Please take your drinks and tell us what is on your mind, Captain," said Mildred.

Sam told them about Caroline's death and how the mystery of it somehow pointed back to the two men who had been recent renters, suspected Nazi Germans whose supposed German activity was beginning to appear more real. Both women were visibly moved at the story of how Caroline had been murdered, and by Nazis, at that.

"How may we be of assistance?" said Agatha.

It was here that Sam's approach really took Officer Perkins by surprise.

"Well, first let me say how lovely your home is," said Sam to the women who graciously accepted his compliment.

Officer Perkins made quick note of Sam's approach. He sensed that Sam was not your ordinary employee of the state. Sam also explained his family background to the group and that his uncle was a war hero who died at Pearl Harbor. It was obvious to the Peet sisters that this state police captain was a man of breeding and wealth. Whatever their intentions were to help before gaining this knowledge went up to a much higher level. For them, Sam was one of their own, the elect. They went from offering information to pledging any assistance they or members of their circle in Milford society could offer. To them, the lovely white cotton gloves of gentility had just come off. When Sam explained that he was the husband of Martha Frost, they were ready for cold compresses. Officer Perkins realized he had no idea who he was dealing with. As far as any sense of humor went, he was sure Sergeant D'Onofrio of the New Haven Police Department had had his own good laugh at this officer's expense.

"I assume you have no idea why both men just disappeared?" Sam began.

"None. No none," said the sisters in unison.

"Would you mind showing me their rooms?" Sam asked.

"Right this way," said Agatha who rose quickly to her feet and headed towards the back stairwell.

The two men had rooms on the second floor that looked directly onto the water. They shared a bathroom. Agatha left Sam alone and instructed him to take all the time he needed. They would keep Officer Perkins company until Sam returned.

It was obvious the two men left in a hurry. Their personal items were gone, but many of their clothes were still here. As Sam inspected the bed of one of the men, he discovered German currency they left behind, tucked between the mattress and bed spring. He could not be guilty of assuming that what he believed was the obvious: Nazis.

Sam was not really sure who these men were. He was soon to find out why they rented these particular rooms, but why either would be in South Carolina, with Caroline, was still a huge mystery.

Back on the sun porch, Sam continued his questioning. "Please tell me a little more about your famous Charles Island," he began.

"Our father is Captain Joshua Peet. Daddy and his partners made their fortune in the shipping business. He always had a fascination for Charles Island. No doubt you have heard the legend of Captain Kidd's treasure. Every community from the Thimble Islands at Stony Point, to Stratford Point, just west of Charles Island, has laid claim to the treasure. Daddy had many contacts and did extensive research at the Yale Library. He also made a friend of the Curator of Antiquities Studies at the New York Public Library, at Bryant Park in Manhattan. Daddy was convinced that the Charles Island story was for real. He also learned that the treasure was reputed to be worth $100 million. I'm sure that amount would draw anyone's attention, especially the Germans to aid their war effort. However, realistic accounts put the treasure, if it does exist, closer to £100,000 sterling. Kidd took to piracy and plundered the French galleon, Quedah Merchant, riding low in the water with her enormous treasure of gold, jewels, silver, artifacts and silk. Who can say how vast the fortune really was?"

The conversation lulled as Sam was trying to take all the information in.

"Tell him about the monks," said Mildred. "Why they came here may not be such a mystery after all."

Sam was intrigued. "Please, Agatha, go on. What is Mildred trying to say?"

"A Dominican Order came here in the late 1920's. When they left, many tunnels and hidden passageways were discovered. No one could figure out why such places were necessary for monks. The monks were a Dominican Order from Hillhouse Avenue, in New Haven. But some of the elder monks were from Bavaria. It is believed they were the ones who encouraged the head of the Order to set up a retreat for young boys, on Charles Island. The monks had made many stops along our coastline before settling on Charles Island. There are stories that they returned to Bavaria after they left and indeed, carried some gold coins back with them. Those coins could be used to convince people of the treasure's existence. All of a sudden, their inexplicable appearance and settling on Charles Island is not so inexplicable, at least, not to me." said Agatha.

Once again, Sam encouraged Agatha to continue. "What is your thinking?" he said.

"I'm thinking that at the very least, those monks felt they had sufficient proof of the treasure to warrant excavation of the island. Up until very recently, the United Illuminating Company had plans to put some sort of power-generating facility out there. And now, all of a sudden, the workers seem to have disappeared just as mysteriously as our two paid guests. I don't know about you, Captain, but that sure smells pretty fishy to me."

Sam eased back in his chair. He marveled at how lucid Agatha's thought process was. Her vast knowledge and articulate rendering really impressed him.

"Martha would love her," he thought.

"I have a suggestion for you," said Agatha.

"What is it?" Sam asked.

"The one chance you have of learning anything more about the retreat, that is real, would be for you to see the Sisters of Lauralton Hall over on High Street. If anyone in the area knows anything about those priests, it would be them. I suggest you make an appointment with the Mother Superior before you go off half-cocked chasing down local folklore tales."

Sam really liked Agatha.

"I'll do just that," he said. I've got to get back to Westbrook, but may come back sometime if that's okay with you."

"Any chance your lovely Mrs. could come with you? Mildred thinks that young lady is the literary 'cat's meow'," said Agatha.

Sam just smiled. "I'll see what I can do." He asked the sisters if they had any paper bags handy, then gathered up all that was left by the two men, and he and Officer Perkins made their exit.

Sam followed the officer to the Post Road, got out to shake his hand and thank him, then made his way north to New Haven, to check in with Matt D'Onofrio and head back home. On the way back to Essex, Sam had a recurring thought that was beginning to give him a headache. Priests, some from Bavaria, in league with Brothers on Hillhouse Avenue, the Skull and Bones in the near vicintity to them, and then a monastery on Charles Island, with Captain Kidd's treasure thrown in; it was beginning to look like things were heading down a path Sam was not looking forward to travel. Yes, a headache was definitely working its way in, but the queasy stomach he was experiencing convinced him that the ride home was sure to be an unpleasant one.

CHAPTER THIRTEEN

Sam briefly broke off his train of thought to say good morning to Aunt Clara who was sitting with Martha at her kitchen table. He made his way over to the stove to pour himself a cup of coffee. He was going through his usual routine which he always seemed to experience at the start of every new case: so many questions and so few answers.

"Why hadn't the other man, Dieter, been seen anywhere?" he wondered. "Was he the killer or was he also dead?" Sam had not gotten any news from Chief White, down in Columbia.

"No news is no news," he groused to himself. And no news was exactly what he did not need, right now.

Shouts of glee shattered Sam's silence as Mary burst into Aunt Clara's kitchen and wrapped her arms around the legs of her surprised father.

"Oh, Daddy, Daddy. I can't believe you and Mommy are going to take me to Lauralton Hall. I am so excited."

Sam had made an appointment to visit the Mother Superior at Lauralton Hall, for Saturday morning. Martha seized the opportunity to go along with him and to bring Mary, who had a strong fascination for the school. Sam agreed, reluctantly.

Sam smiled down at Mary. "Okay. Okay, young lady," he said. Saturday is still a few days away. You still have a couple of days of school, right? Don't want to get yourself all in an uproar over this. Business as usual until Saturday, okay?"

"Oh Daddy," said Mary in a tone of exasperation. "Mommy," she said as she turned to Martha, "you had better have a talk with him."

With that, Mary turned and skipped out of the house to join Thomas and Lilith on the lawn.

"Mary thinks she wants to go there for high school," said Martha.

"That's at least a forty-five minute train ride, with no delays," said Sam. "That would add at least two hours to her school day."

Sam noticed a strange look on Martha's face. "You are smiling. Why are you smiling?" He said.

Martha realized there was no easy way of telling him. "Lauralton Hall is a boarding school for privileged girls," she said.

"What!" Sam exploded.

Martha threw her hands up to try to calm him down. "Now Sam, please try not to get too excited by this. Mary has only just started the sixth grade. We have three years before we come to that juncture.

A lot can happen in that time, believe me. But you have to acknowledge that Lauralton Hall is a direct gateway to the Ivy League, and Yale is in the Ivy League. Mary is an extraordinary student. Let's wait and see how things turn out. The worst thing you could do is to try to discourage her. That would put Mary in a very awkward position. She would never do anything that you did not approve of. I'm not so sure we should put that kind of pressure on her, right now, and anyway, she would be home every weekend."

Martha's words made sense, but this new revelation was almost too much for Sam to contend with. Mary's going away to college, even if only to New Haven, was one thing for him to accept. But, the thought of her going away for high school? Once again, Sam's stomach was experiencing some problems.

CHAPTER FOURTEEN

The rest of the week went pretty much without incident. Sam tried to busy himself with his regular duties with the state police, but things were unexpectedly quiet on the home front, leaving Sam to stew over so many unanswered questions. He found himself actually looking forward to Saturday, and meeting with the Sisters of Lauralton Hall.

Traffic along the Post Road on Saturday morning, was a little more crowded than usual. The weather was all sunshine which probably added to the allure of folks heading out early for the beaches. Labor Day had come and gone, but the weather was still warm and inviting, and folks were not going to resist taking every opportunity to enjoy it. It took a full hour to reach Milford. Sam made a left hand turn onto High Street, heading towards the town green and Lauralton Hall.

As soon as Sam turned right onto the school grounds and passed through the large iron gates, he and the family were met by the majestic presence of Lauralton Hall, sitting regally at the center of the forty-acre, perfectly manicured property, on which it was located. Sam had to admit to himself that the site was most impressive. Martha had that all-knowing look of satisfaction that she possessed so well on her face. Mary was beyond words.

Lauralton Hall was once the residence of James Augustine Taylor, a millionaire who many believe named the house after his beloved daughter, Laura, who died at an early age. Taylor lived there until his death in 1899, and left a fortune of $20 million, a sum that would have made him a billionaire by mid-20th century standards.

Taylor was quite a controversial character. After his first wife, Mary, passed away he married a second, Elizabeth, who later filed for divorce citing his many affairs, including one with his housekeeper with whom he had a child. He bequeathed the housekeeper, Louise Katherine Duvernoy, $20,000 upon his death, a sum itself, that would be valued at $1 million by the same standard.

Taylor was a major benefactor to the town of Milford. He deeded the land on Milford Green to the United Methodist Church and donated a large sum of money to the church, in honor of the memory of his first wife, Mary. He also contributed a large amount of money to the construction of the Milford Library, an impressive stone building on the northernmost end of the Milford Green. He seemed to be a complex man of many inconsistencies, a characteristic consistent with men of great wealth of that period.

Whatever scandal or shame the owner of Lauralton Hall bore, it did not deter the Sisters of Mercy, originally from Meriden, from purchasing the property and turning it into a highly regarded educational institution for young women.

Sam was escorted by one of the Sisters to the office of the Mother Superior, while the other took Martha and Mary on a tour of the main school building which was as impressive as the original structure.

It was immediately apparent that the magnificent main house had been perfectly preserved. The Sisters of Mercy had seen to that. The main house served as administration and business offices, as well as living quarters for the Sisters in residence. The St. Joseph's building, constructed in 1905, provided classrooms for the girls, as well as boarding and dining accommodations for the students who came from great distances or whose well-heeled parents were content to ship them off, allowing those parents to pursue their busy business and social lives.

The architecture of St. Joseph's, a three-storied structure, paid faithful homage to that of the manor house to which it was attached, and to the period of its origin. Sam immediately identified with the atmosphere of peaceful reverence. There was an unmistakable sense of order that flowed through the halls. Even before he met the Mother Superior, Sam got the feeling that Lauralton Hall was about serious Catholic education.

"Hello Captain, I am Sister Mary Evelyn. Welcome to Lauralton Hall," said the Mother Superior. "How may I be of assistance to you?"

Even Sam was not sure of the answer to that question. "I'll be honest, Sister, I'd have to call this visit a shot in the dark," said Sam. "My daughter, Mary, is infatuated with your school, so my wife and I decided they should come along. I am grateful to you for receiving us on such short notice."

"Well, the school tour is easy for us," said the Mother Superior with a smile, "but again, why do you come to me?"

"I was told that you might be able to shed some light on the religious order at Charles Island," said Sam.

"Aquinas," said Sister Mary Evelyn with an air of annoyance as she plopped down in her chair. She bade Sam do the same.

"Not such happy memories?" said Sam.

"I'd have to say that you could say fifty-fifty in the happy memories department," said the Sister.

Sam gave her a quizzical look, without asking her to elaborate. He didn't need to.

"The Brothers from the order in New Haven, were wonderful; the ones from Bavaria . . ." she let the words hang.

"Not so wonderful?" Sam asked.

"They were pushy and boorish," she responded. "But they picked the right order to align themselves with. The Brothers from New Haven, bent over backwards to make amends for their actions. Those Brothers truly had the love of Christ in their hearts. Believe me, they needed it with that group."

"Your candor is surprising," said Sam.

"We are a religious order, Captain, one dedicated to serve God's people. We took an oath to follow the tenets of our faith. We had no need for the Bavarian Brothers making things difficult for us.

These are troubled times, and people look to us for comfort. That group walked around like the ancient Pharisees, expecting people to genuflect at their very presence. And one more thing, I could never get beyond the thought that they bore a distinct dislike for America. They treated the locals with contempt. I found that strange, even suspicious. Some years ago I was able to spend time in Rome, and I found their actions and attitude totally out of step with Holy Mother Church."

"So you could accept the belief that they might be in sympathy with the Nazis and their cause?" said Sam.

The Sister took a few seconds to think about it and then responded. "Yes, now that you mention it. As a matter of fact, that could go a long way towards explaining their behavior. But, tell me Captain, why does a state police Captain from Westbrook travel down here to inquire about a group of Bavarian clergy?"

Sam told the Sister the story of the murder of his cousin in South Carolina, and how the trail led back to Milford, and quite possibly a hunt by Germany for buried treasure on Charles Island. If that were the case, it was plausible to assume that the Bavarian Order might have some part in their plans.

Sister Mary Evelyn was touched by the shocking details of Caroline Tyler's murder, but she had pretty much told Sam all she could. It was for no other reason, but that she simply did not know anything else concerning the whereabouts and actions of the Bavarian Brothers. The abandoning of the Dominican's Aquinas facility, so without warning, was as much a mystery to her as anyone else. She took Sam on an abbreviated tour of the manor house, before going over to the St. Joseph's School Building to meet up with Martha and Mary.

※   ※   ※

Sam checked in with the barracks in Westbrook, and then took the girls in tow to meet up with Lizzy Childers at Consiglio's on Wooster Street, in New Haven. Sam loved the old world charm of one of New Haven's most revered Italian restaurants.

"Daddy, there is a chapel on the third floor," Mary exclaimed. "An honest-to-goodness chapel, can you believe it?"

"So, you really liked Lauralton Hall." Sam asked, knowing all too well what the answer was.

"Oh Daddy, said Mary, "I just loved it."

Sam looked over at Martha who could do nothing but offer a sympathetic look back.

"Three years," said Sam to himself, over and over again.

Halfway through their meal, Sam was informed that he had a phone call. He excused himself and went to the reception desk. He returned ten minutes later. Martha immediately recognized the look on his face.

"Trouble?" she said.

"I'm afraid so," said Sam. "Lizzy, would you mind entertaining my two ladies here while I take a trip back to Milford? I promise to be back as soon as possible."

"Don't rush on my account," said Lizzy. Martha and Mary erupted in laughter. "I want to hear all about Lauralton Hall from Mary. You take your time. We'll be just fine."

Sam took Martha outside to tell her the news. "That was a message from Officer Perkins down in Milford. It seems a Naval Intelligence Officer was found murdered in the Morningside section of Woodmont, in Milford. Police questioned some of the guests at the establishment and one of them is missing. He fits the description of Wilhelm Dieter."

Sam was going to meet Matt D'Onofrio at New Haven police department. The Sergeant knew the terrain well and could get them quickly to the Milford crime scene. The death of a naval intelligence officer, especially during wartime, was very serious business. Sam knew that the State Department would be coming into this affair and he would be counted on to lend assistance, as Milford fell within his jurisdiction. It also allowed him free reign to plow into the investigation, officially. For the moment, anyway, things were beginning to look up.

CHAPTER FIFTEEN

The Soundview Guest Hotel sat high on a bluff overlooking Long Island Sound, in Morningside. Sam and Matt exited the cruiser and walked up the front walkway to meet up with Officer Perkins, who was waiting for them on the front porch. Many of the guests were milling around, trying to get as much information as they could. Summers in Milford were boom time. A great deal of the economy depended on the season between Memorial Day and Labor Day. A murder of suspicious origin could cause havoc for the local economy. Sam would later learn that a murder might be right up the alley, as they would say, for those who would do anything to add to the town's folklore.

Officer Perkins led the two policeman back to the room in which the naval officer had been killed. The room had been rented out to Wilhelm Dieter.

"Why hadn't Perkins mentioned that when he called me?" Sam asked himself. That little omission started to create some reservations in Sam's mind concerning Officer Perkins' professionalism. Sam had gone down this road before with a certain officer in Old Saybrook, and realizing the outcome of that situation, he decided to cut Perkins some slack while keeping a careful eye on him.

"That clears one thing up for me," said Sam. Before the others could ask what he meant, Sam offered, "It looks like Dieter is our man for the South Carolina murders. Either that or he is part of a small group bent on covering their tracks."

"Have you or anyone else ever seen Dieter or Kempler in the company of anyone else during their stay?" Matt D'Onofrio asked Officer Perkins.

"No," said Perkins. "I know I never have, and since my meeting up with Captain Tyler, here, I've been doing some digging around. Nobody I have talked to has ever seen anything but the two of them together, alone."

Perkins' revelation was already causing Sam to reevaluate his position as far as that police officer was concerned. "It stands to reason those two worked alone; less chance of drawing attention to themselves," said Sam. "If there were any other parties, it could have compromised their plans to carry out whatever they intended to do, without drawing suspicion."

Matt D'Onofrio agreed. Both men looked down at the body of the naval intelligence officer who had been stabbed many times. They were informed that it would take at least twenty-four hours for the coroner to establish the exact number of times he was stabbed, and if stabbing was the cause of death.

"If Dieter did this, it's a good bet he carries a certain amount of anger while doing his job," said Sam. "This guy is dangerous. Make sure you make all law enforcement agencies aware of that. We don't want any of our people walking blindly into harm's way. It appears this guy might even enjoy his work, no matter how bloody or treacherous it is. That will not bode well for anyone with whom he has issues."

Sam told Officer Perkins to call him with every new detail, no matter how small or seemingly insignificant. He knew the State Department boys would be watching him closely. The Navy was not going to be too happy to learn that they would not be taking part in the investigation. It would only be a matter of hours before the victim's commanding officer would be contacting Sam. Sam expected some early rough going; for sure. The fact that Sam had never served in the military was not going to ingratiate him to the commanding officer. Sam knew he was about to experience a whole new level of chain of command and of answering to authority.

Sam and Matt walked over to the sea wall with Officer Perkins. The view was magnificent. The sky was crystal clear, offering an amazing view of Long Island, some 27 miles across the sound.

"Wow," said Sam, pointing down at a 45° angle, to a large home about half a mile across an inlet. "Who lives in that place?"

Officer Perkins let out a laugh. "I was wondering if you would notice that place. That, my friend, is the Villa Rosa, owned by the late Sylvester Poli, the movie house king. And those," he said, while pointing to 10 more homes, smaller versions of the Villa Rosa, stretching over a private crescent parcel of land with a private beach, "are the Poli Cottages for family and guests. The sons and the Poli Trust own them all. The old man died a few years ago. He built that beautiful home for his wife and named it after her. He left a huge fortune behind. Kind of looks like pure Hollywood with some Newport thrown in, doesn't it?" Perkins said.

"Like I said, 'Wow'," said Sam. "Who lives there now?"

"One of the sons, I believe. There seems to be a lot of renovation going on, workers coming day and night. Nobody knows what they're doing. The son keeps to himself. Not much of a talker when he goes out. Actually he rarely goes out. He's sort of a recluse. He's friendly enough, just not much of a talker. Remember, these are theatrical people. I think he enjoys wearing a cloak of mystery. Probably thinks that makes him attractive to the females. Goodness knows, there are a whole lot of half-naked bodies walking around Milford beaches in the summer."

Sam took Matt back to the New Haven Police Station, then headed on over to the Wooster Street area to collect Martha and Mary. He did a quick ten minute catch-up with Lizzy's husband Peter, then headed home with two now very tired ladies. But, his day was far from over. Just about the time they hit Saybrook, his police phone rang. It was a call from Commander Anthony Thomas of the U.S. Navy. The commander had been in touch with the Governor, to get clearance to deal directly with Sam. His directive caught Sam by surprise.

"Be at the Quinnipiac Terminal in New Haven Harbor, at midnight, sharp," were his orders. "I will send officers there with a launch to take you to my headquarters."

Once again, Sam was surprised, because as far as he knew, there was no Navy presence in the area of Milford. He put in a call to Matt D'Onofrio who was of the same understanding. Sam waved off his friend's offer to meet him at the New Haven Harbor. Sam did not anticipate any problems. He did, however, put in a call to the Governor's office to see if the commander was for real. About an hour later he got a return call from the Governor's right-hand man, one whose voice Sam knew well, informing him that the meeting was indeed sanctioned by the Governor. So instead of sharing a warm bed with his new wife, Sam was about to experience the cool breezes of Long Island Sound, compliments of the U.S. Navy.

CHAPTER SIXTEEN

Sam turned the motor of his police vehicle off. It was exactly 12 midnight, and he could see two Naval officers dead ahead of him, standing at the pier. He made his way over to them and showed his identification and badge. The Navy men gestured for him to join them in their craft, a very ordinary 18—foot outboard that anyone might own. It was not what Sam expected. When he inquired as to why this particular boat, he was told that it was the only type that could navigate the waters of the area they were headed for. Sam could sense that neither of these two escorts was going to be very forth—coming. Their demeanor gave him a good idea of what he could expect their commanding officer's personality to be: cold, abrupt and lacking in social graces. This was not going to be tea with the Peet sisters.

The officer guiding the boat held a steady, medium speed, southwesterly course, towards Milford. Sam was not at all familiar with this area. After about 20 minutes, the boat slowed and made a right turn towards the shoreline. All at once Sam noticed a blinking signal coming from straight in front of the boat. Sam judged it to be about 200 feet away. The boat made a slow, deliberate approach, then slowed even more. Sam could see a gazebo sitting on top of a stone wall with a bridge made of stone leading to the main property. He had only seen this house once, and for a very brief time, but he was absolutely sure that they were at the Villa Rosa.

The boat slowed even more but kept heading for the blinking light and stone wall. Sam was a little apprehensive, as it appeared they were going to crash right into it. To his utter amazement and relief, Sam realized that they had entered a passageway through the wall leading under the property. Sylvester Poli had constructed a boathouse and pier directly under the Villa Rosa. Officer Perkins was right when he summed up the Poli family as theatrical. The tunnel was about 50 feet deep. The officers secured the boat and instructed Sam to get out and follow them.

Sam was led to a large room, probably one serving as a cellar and storage area. But now, it was brightly lit up with walls of radio equipment. Sam immediately found himself standing face to face with Commander Anthony Thomas, chief officer of this operation.

"Thank you for coming on such short notice, Captain Tyler," said Commander Thomas.

"No problem," said Sam. "How may I be of service to you?"

The Commander gestured for Sam to take a seat and offered him some coffee.

"I did some checking up on you and learned that you lost an uncle on the Arizona. Allow me to express my condolences. A lot of good men went down at Pearl. From what I have been able to gather, you have done your uncle proud, right here on American soil. I'll be perfectly honest, Captain, I was not thrilled to be left out of the loop as far as the investigation goes, but I have been assured by Washington that you are the best man to go forward with the investigation. The Navy simply cannot spare anyone to do it at this time. We are fortunate to have you so close by, to represent us."

Sam accepted the commander's kind words and filled him in on the death of his cousin with Dieter's partner. Sam had been looking for Dieter, and now was convinced that this affair had Nazi Germany and espionage written all over it. Sam made it very clear that this was not only his job, but that this was personal. The fact that there was the distinct possibility that something very threatening to the country was at hand, only made him more resolved to do whatever he had to do, to find out what was going on and to put an end to it. The commander grasped Sam's intent. He was pleased with what he heard.

"Agent Lipton noticed a man at the Villa Rosa gates one day. He just assumed that he was an inquisitive summer vacationer. But then he noticed someone up on Morningside, just sitting and watching the Villa Rosa. Lipton went to a room upstairs, and with his binoculars, saw that the man was also using binoculars to observe the Villa, and that he was making notes. A couple of days later, the man was seen on an outboard coming close to the property. The guy was dressed like a businessman. He didn't even have sense enough to wear appropriate clothing to avoid suspicion. A few days later, a visitor at a guesthouse saw him walking on the private beach at low tide, and asked what he was doing there. The man got nervous and made a hasty retreat, then disappeared. When he reported it to us, we learned that the man matched the description of the man we had been observing.

Agent Lipton took a chance and began to observe the activity up at the Soundview Hotel. We have a signal tower located behind the fire station up there. No one would suspect its purpose. Maybe Dieter did. Agent Lipton discovered that this Dieter fellow was a guest at the hotel. Our best guess is Dieter lured him to his room and murdered him. We are of the opinion that this Dieter character is a certified killer. Not much on brains, but more than willing to kill. It might work in our favor if he really is that arrogant, to think he can just come here and do this without even trying to mask his intentions. Whoever picked him probably did not do it for his IQ. If he is responsible for the South Carolina murders, he is someone to consider very dangerous.

Sam agreed. He and the Commander spent about an hour together. They talked about the war and how things were going. Sam also filled him in on the Charles Island connection. The Commander knew all about Charles Island and its fabled treasure. He told Sam that his job was to monitor Long Island Sound water activity, and to coordinate the efforts of the Navy and the Coast Guard, to keep the water free of enemy ships. Sam learned that all the activity around the mansion was a ruse to mask the Navy's presence and purpose for being there. Dieter seemed to have figured that out. Maybe he wasn't so stupid after all.

The tide was still high, the reason for the meeting at midnight. Low tide made it impossible to access the underground tunnel. Sam was taken back to New Haven Harbor, to collect his car, then he headed home. He finally crawled into bed a little after 2 AM. He never heard Martha ask how things went. He was out, the moment his head touched the pillow.

CHAPTER SEVENTEEN

The sun was shining through the curtains, greeting Sam's resistant eyes. He reached over to his left and realized he was alone in bed. Glancing over to the clock on his nightstand with half-focused eyes, he could barely make out that it was 8:30. He also realized it was Sunday morning.

He quickly got up, showered and made his way down to the kitchen. No one was there. He saw a note on the table informing him that everyone was over at Aunt Clara's having breakfast and that the ten o'clock service at St. Peter's, was in less than an hour. Sam ran back upstairs to get dressed. He noticed that his clothes were laid out for him. He quickly dressed and made his way across the lawn, to Aunt Clara's. Mercifully, coffee was waiting for him along with his family.

"Well good morning, Sunshine," came Aunt Clara's cheery greeting.

Sam just muttered something unintelligible.

"How was your midnight visit, honey?" said Martha.

"Nautical," said Sam. "I'll fill you in later. And speaking of filling, is there anything here left for poor old dad to eat?" he spoke in the direction of his children.

"Sit down, and I'll fix you a plate of pancakes and eggs," said Aunt Clara.

Thirty minutes later they were entering St. Peter's Episcopal Church for the 10 o'clock service with Reverend Foster.

＊　　＊　　＊

Sam pulled into the Templeton's driveway at 11:30. The children were going to have lunch and spend the rest of the day with their grandparents. Arlen Templeton met everyone at the side entrance and gave his grandchildren big hugs, then sent them into the house to see their Grandmother Betty.

"You look tired, Son," said Arlen.

"It shows that much?" Sam said.

"Come on, let's have some coffee and have a chat. I have been waiting for you to come over," said Arlen.

With little prodding, Sam began to fill Arlen in on the past few weeks, and the murders he was now entrusted to solve.

"So sorry to hear about Caroline; she was a sweet child. Clara must be devastated," said Arlen.

"Yes," said Sam, "but she never lets that get in the way of duty. We will be giving Caroline a memorial service, two weeks from yesterday. As soon as we can work it out, Martha is going with her to Hawaii, to scatter Caroline's ashes at Pearl Harbor. She and Aunt Clara have gotten very close."

"You did well, Son," said Arlen. "Betty and I are so happy for you. The children tell us all about how wonderful Martha is to them. I'm sure our Sally is smiling down on us. But tell me, what's on your mind? I think I can be of some help if you will let me."

"Well," Sam started, "it appears that two Nazi agents have been sent on a mission here. Actually, down in Milford. One is dead; and the other appears to be a murderer. It is very possible the other one is also responsible for the death of his partner, and Cousin Caroline down in South Carolina. The actions of these two lead me to believe that they were sent here to see if the story of the hidden treasure on Charles Island, off the coast of Milford, is true."

"Captain Kidd and the $100 million booty," said Arlen.

"You know about that?" Sam said.

"I'm a millionaire, Son. Any story that talks about great amounts of money is something I am interested in. And $100 million is a great amount of money. But, although the story is intriguing, I have been assured by the best geologists that any attempts to dig out there would prove disastrous. I don't doubt a treasure exists and that it is there; I just don't think anyone is ever going to be able to access it. Believe me, if I thought otherwise, my people would have been out there," said Arlen. "Is there anything else?"

"Yes," said Sam. "It seems that there is a secret U.S. Navy station in Milford."

"The Villa Rosa," said Arlen.

That stopped Sam in his tracks. "You know about the Villa Rosa?"

Arlen let out a laugh. "I know a whole lot about a lot of things, Sam. I have a lot of friends in high places. And I'll tell you what my friends know—they can trust me. Trust is everything in times like these. These people know I love my country and I will do anything I can to ensure its safety. And I will tell you what I know—I can trust you, and I do, implicitly."

Sam was quiet for a moment. Both men just stood there.

"You are a good man, Arlen," said Sam. "I saw so much of you in Sally. So please help me out here. I need to know why the Sound is so important to the Navy, and what significance a Bavarian religious order has in all this. My only guess is somehow the Illuminati has something to do with the two Nazi agents and their mission, and why the Bavarians chose to be part of an order out of New Haven, where the Skulls just happened to be located. It's a popular belief that the Skulls and the Illuminati have very close ties. If this is true, here we go again."

Arlen paused for a moment, then said, "Before you go too far with that line of reasoning, let me jot down the name of someone whom I believe you should talk to."

"Who is it?" Sam said.

"Whitney Broome, the new advisor to the Skulls. He is a good man, Sam. It would be wise to inform him of your suspicions as far as the Illuminati and the Germans are concerned, and any possible connection to the Skull and Bones. I truly believe he would have none of that. His family is passionate about this country."

Arlen could see that Sam was becoming frustrated. "I have the name of another person I think you should see. His name is William Abbott. You'll find him down in Bridgeport. Abbott can fill in a lot of the spaces for you. I'll put a call into him to set up a meeting. He's a Princeton man, but a darn good American. He runs that giant General Electric plant down there. The man knows everything about that neck of the woods. Sit tight, I'll get to him first thing tomorrow. Relax, Sam, I know you'll catch these guys."

"I'm getting the feeling that Dieter might just disappear. I don't think he was meant to be here alone. I'll be waiting for your call," said Sam.

Sam went into the house to say hello to Betty, and goodbye to the kids. He and Arlen shook hands, then Sam headed home to tell Martha all that had transpired. It'd been a while since Martha and Sam had some time alone. It was a warm, beautiful Sunday afternoon, just right for holding hands and leisurely walks. Sam told Martha about the underground naval base at Villa Rosa and his conversation with Arlen. He could see the look in Martha's eyes.

"Another book?" he said.

"Just think about it," said Martha, "German spies, Nazis, the Illuminati, murder, a secret naval installation, Captain Kidd's treasure on an island filled with mystery—my head is spinning."

"You are not planning to involve yourself in any way in this, are you?" Sam said.

"Not if you make me a promise, Husband" she said. "Promise to share everything with me. Everything. I'll take notes so I can start a story line for my next book. I knew marrying you was a good idea; great for my career."

"Really," said Sam as he drew her close and kissed her, right in front of the Black Swan.

Just then, Wanda Loomis came out to scold them. "Have some decency, you two," she said as the three stood there and shared a laugh. The mood was quickly broken.

The door to the Black Swan opened and Allison Tinsley exited on the arm of her new beau. At first, everyone stood in awkward silence.

"Samuel Tyler," said Sam as he extended his hand to Allison's man.

"Lawrence Mulcahy," was the man's response as he took Sam's hand. ""I finally get to meet you, Captain Tyler."

Again, there was silence. Allison did not say a word. She just stood there looking as though she had just scored a great victory.

"This is my wife, Martha," said Sam, once again breaking the silence.

"A pleasure, Mrs. Tyler. My sister loves your books. She's dying for the next one to come out," said Mulcahy. "Well, have a pleasant day, folks," he said as he took Allison's arm and led her north up Main Street.

Sam, Martha and Wanda went inside. "I feel like dessert," said Sam. He ordered the Black Swan's famous apple cranberry cobbler with vanilla ice cream, and whipped cream on top. He and Martha would share one.

Wanda served them and sat down, uninvited.

"Well," she said. "What do you make of that?"

Sam just smiled. "An unlikely couple, I have to admit. But Allison has always been willful. No one could ever tell what she would do next. That's why her mother was so willing to leave her behind with the mayor, when she vamoosed. The mayor's family paid a lot of money to that woman to stay away, and she was not about to share it with a 14 year-old, loose cannon of a daughter."

CHAPTER EIGHTEEN

Martha finished her regularly scheduled two hour, Monday morning lecture-hall session and headed towards the campus parking lot. She had taken charge of Sam's Buick sedan. There was a three-hour break before her next class. Time enough to head over to the Yale library. She was determined to get as much material on the Illuminati as possible.

Martha showed her Albertus Magnus badge to the library receptionist, and made her way to the card file. Within ten minutes she had five books dedicated solely to Adam Weishaupt and the Illuminati. As she pored over the material, she began to realize that the basic beliefs of this clandestine group, the abolishing of church and governmental rule, in favor of a select group totally in charge of all society, was just what Hitler was all about. No church, monarchy or elected officials were to have any power to govern, whatsoever. She concluded that Adolf Hitler bought into that idea, hook line and sinker.

It was a common belief that Hitler drew inspiration from the Spanish Inquisition, thus his use of those terrible gas chambers to exterminate the Jews. Martha was convinced that the beliefs of the Illuminati had influenced him just as profoundly.

Suddenly, she felt a strange sensation. She sat up and looked around the room. Off in a distant corner she caught sight of a man who seemed to be watching her. Their eyes met, but the man did not look away. Finally, he turned and left. Martha made a few more notes and then headed back over to the section where all the books concerning the Illuminati were kept. As she reached for one of the volumes, she looked to her left to see the man once again staring at her, but this time he was only ten or so feet away. He took a step towards her, but halted when Martha spoke to him.

"Who are you and what do you want?" she asked.

The man merely smiled and cautiously took another step towards her. He was not very tall or physically imposing, but Martha knew instinctively that his mood was threatening. Quickly, she grabbed the biggest books she could get her hands on and threw them at the intruder.

"What do you want?" she yelled, catching the attention of all the people within earshot. The man turned and made a hasty retreat. By the time the security people showed up, he was long gone.

Matt D'Onofrio was on the scene in less than thirty minutes, followed by Sam, thirty minutes later. By the time Sam got there, Matt was pretty sure that the intruder fit the description of Dieter perfectly. He and Sam were really baffled. Why would Dieter have any interest in Martha? How did he even know about Martha?

Sam had to consider the possibility that this was an attack on his family. He was ready to dismiss the notion as totally implausible, but everything about this case was appearing totally implausible. As of right now, Sam was beginning to get the feeling that whoever was behind this, was either quite brilliant or totally insane. In either case, Sam was getting nowhere fast. It was not something he was feeling very good about. He had to wonder, if this was an attack on Martha, could the children be next? All of a sudden, Sam was realizing the vulnerability of his family. He also realized that he had to act fast. He knew he could not sustain a long investigation and be able to protect Aunt Clara and the children. He put in a call to Arlen Templeton who assured Sam of immediate help. From this point, the children would no longer go anywhere unless escorted by Sam or Arlen's private security people. Whoever foolishly thought up this plan, obviously had no idea they would be inviting Arlen Templeton and his vast resources to the party. Still, the fact remained, this could not be a long drawn out affair.

Sam knew that he had the resources of the United States Government at his disposal, but he was going to make sure that they were used judiciously. When he was sure of what course of action to take, he would pull out all the stops.

CHAPTER NINTEEN

The elevator, operated by ladies wearing white gloves, took Martha and Sam to the top floor of the D.M. Reads Department Store, in downtown Bridgeport. The doors opened to one of the most elegant of restaurants, the famous Venetian Tea Room with its sumptuous interior and amazing view of Long Island Sound. The receptionist led them to the table of a waiting William Abbott.

Sam had convinced Martha to cancel her scheduled classes and come with him to meet Arlen's friend. Sam had called the chancellor at Albertus Magnus, to explain that considering the possibility of danger, Martha should take a few days off. The chancellor was in full agreement. Of course, Sam had another, more personal motive; he was not about to let Martha out of his sight anymore than he had to.

Abbott stood and greeted them, and a round of drinks was ordered. Sam and Martha ordered iced tea; Abbott chose scotch. During lunch, Abbott filled the Tylers in on all of the manufacturing activity that was taking place in and around Bridgeport. The General Electric Company operated one of the largest manufacturing facilities in the world. The list of products they produced was staggering. Close by was Afco Lycoming, on the water in neighboring Stratford, where airplane engines were being produced. Remington Arms, the giant munitions manufacturer, was right across the street from G.E. Both companies shared a railway spur that connected them to the New York, New Haven and Hartford railway system and to Bridgeport's deep harbor. In fact, Bridgeport had a vast railway network that connected all manufacturing companies together. Sikorsky Aircraft, which produced helicopters, was located just behind Seaside Park, a two-mile stretch of one of the finest beaches in the northeast. It was once the backyard of P.T. Barnum's Marina Estate. Remington Rand, Dictaphone, Singer Sewing Machines, Hubble Electric, Bridgeport Brass and many more, all took part in the manufacturing of war machinery, operating double and sometimes triple shifts. All were in direct vicinity and had access to each other.

Before dessert and cordials were consumed, Abbott pulled out a map of the Bridgeport area, and spread it out on the table.

"It's pretty impressive, don't you think?" Abbott said, referring to the ingenious layout of industry, all along the coastline, and interconnected by a rail system.

Sam had to agree. It was one of the most efficient complexes he had ever seen. He was beginning to have a whole new appreciation for the city of the bridges, which was really a city of factories.

"Only one problem," Abbott said.

Sam and Martha just looked at him, wondering what he was referring to. Just then, Martha noticed a large circle on the map that had no title or markings.

"What is this circle?" she asked.

Abbott sat back and smiled. "I want to show you folks something. Would you mind coming with me over to the windows?"

The three got up and went over to the windows overlooking Long Island Sound. After a few seconds, Abbott was convinced his guests saw nothing out of the ordinary. He asked them to get as close to the windows as possible and then directed their attention to look as far to the left as they could turn. There, about a mile away, was a huge ten-story storage tank, sitting right off the harbor.

"That tank, my friends, holds millions of gallons of gas. Should a submarine get into the sound and bomb it, well, you can just kiss Bridgeport and Stratford and Fairfield, goodbye. As well as the loss of thousands of lives, the war effort would be severely crippled. And now you know why the Navy is in Milford. Besides the Navy, there is never a time when the skies are free from surveillance. The Army and Air Force operate many different types of crafts to monitor the skies discreetly, from Montauk to Whitestone. There is a constant surveillance. Both Bridgeport and Stratford have multiple gas storage facilities. They would surely add to the catastrophic consequences should those tanks blow. So you see why the Nazi spies might come here to try to devise a plan to do just that. If air and sea attacks are ruled out, they would have to come up with a plan for a land operation."

Things were beginning to become much clearer to Sam. He and Martha had coffee, while Abbott had a little sherry. They thanked him for his time and a lovely lunch. Martha could see that Sam could not wait to get to the car to tell her what he was thinking. She was just as anxious. If her book about the murders in Essex was going to be a bestseller, this new book was sure to be a whopper. Of course, she was counting on her husband to make sure that there would be a story to write.

"The real reason for Dieter and Kempler being here was to confirm that the Navy is here monitoring the sound," he said.

"The treasure theory was just to create a diversion to mask their real purpose for being here," said Martha.

"And if there is a treasure, well, that's just an added bonus," said Sam.

"And, if they could accomplish both, that would surely be a feather in their caps. Whoever sent them here would really appreciate that," said Martha. "But how does Caroline fit into all of this?"

"Believe it or not," said Sam, "that's easy. Something went wrong. Something must have happened to create a rift between the two men. Kempler must have done something to upset Dieter, so much so that he followed him all the way to South Carolina, to do nothing else but kill him. The only thing I could think of that would cause something like that to happen, would be a loose tongue.

"Honey, slow down, you are getting too excited. Remember, this is not a police vehicle and you're going pretty fast," said Martha.

Sam had a laugh. "Yeah," he said, "at this rate we'll be home in twenty minutes, that is if we don't get pulled over for speeding in every town along the way."

Of course, Martha was right. They had chosen to take the Buick that day. Getting stopped for speeding could have been embarrassing for Sam. Martha was just happy to see the fires starting to get ignited in Sam's investigative mind. Sam was really on to something; she could sense it. As they went over the Devon drawbridge connecting Stratford to Milford, on US#1, Sam noticed a Milford Police vehicle approaching them with lights flashing. He pulled over and waited as the Milford Police Officer got out and came towards them.

"Captain Tyler?" he inquired.

"Yes," said Sam. "What is it, Officer?"

"Got your plate from Sargeant D'Onofrio, in New Haven. We have been trying to locate you, Sir, for about an hour. Officer Perkins asked me to tell you that the body of a female washed up near Bayview. Officer Perkins says he has some information for you. Please follow me."

Sam agreed and followed the officer through town, past Point Lookout towards Morningside. It took less than ten minutes. He told Martha to wait in the car until he knew what was going on. He got out and walked over to Officer Perkins, who was standing over a body covered with a police blanket. Perkins bent over and lifted the blanket off the corpse. The salt water and rocks where she was found did not make her a pretty sight.

"Mary Lou Donavan, a thirty-five year old barfly who hangs out at the Beachcomber, a regular bucket of blood, in Bayview," was how Perkins described the victim. "She was discovered hours ago, but we're still waiting for the New Haven coroner's people to get here. I decided to call them instead of the local boys because one of the guys who found her—he was fishing off the rocks—remembers her getting into a real brawl with some guy who was not from around here. He said she was calling him a lying Kraut. Kraut is a slang term for German. They say the guy was laughing and dragged her out of the place by her hair. It seems to be a common occurrence in that establishment. No one intervened. Considering the condition of the patrons, I doubt anyone could have, even if they tried."

As Perkins was talking, Sam motioned for Martha to join them. She heard most of the conversation; she just stared at Sam.

"You knew," she said.

Now it was Perkins' turn to just stand there and stare.

"Did they remember anything else?" Sam said.

"Captain, you're lucky they even remembered that night."

Sam thanked Officer Perkins and told him he would be in touch. He was going to the New Haven PD, if anything else should come up. He and Martha took their leave.

"Dieter killed that woman and probably attempted to kill Kempler, who somehow got away. I think Kempler knew it would just be a matter of time before Dieter would kill him, so he ran. Dieter is the killer, not Kempler. Kempler's appetite for the ladies got him killed. If what I'm thinking turns out to be the truth, then we have another problem."

Martha didn't ask. She just waited for Sam to say what was on his mind.

"There is a third party, someone with money," he said. "Someone who could find Kempler and send Dieter to kill him. I don't like to think this, but the Skulls could do that, especially if this Illuminati thing is real."

CHAPTER TWENTY

No sooner had Martha and Sam reached the steps to the New Haven Police Department, they were met by Matt D'Onofrio. "I need some coffee," he said.

When Sam motioned they go inside, Matt said, "Not that 'swill'. Come, my friends, I'm going to introduce you two to a whole new world of coffee drinking."

Matt took them over to Willoughby's on Chapel Street, right across from the Yale campus where they roast coffee on the premises. Coffee-lovers from all over the world know about Willoughby's. If you live on this planet, Willoughby ships to you. If you visited anywhere in the area, you made a special visit to Willoughby's. Travelers from New York to Boston, would call ahead and be met at the New Haven Train Station by their delivery boys.

It was a beautiful summer afternoon and the three friends sat at the outdoor café. It seemed that half the people walking along Chapel Street knew the sergeant. Sam filled Matt in on all that had happened both in Bridgeport and Milford.

"Wow, that's some story," said Matt. "Sam, see if this makes a lot of sense. I got to thinking about Martha's little experience the other day. Now

Martha, don't get upset; this is just a theory, a good theory, but still, just a theory."

Martha sat up straight and looked right into Matt's eyes. Somehow, she sensed she was not going to like what she heard.

"Peter Childers," said Matt.

No sooner had the words left his lips than Martha sprang to her feet. Sam gently sat her back down.

"Come on, honey, at least hear what Matt has to say," said Sam. Sam motioned for Matt to continue.

"Childers has a number of students who meet at his home. Some just happen to be Skulls. Everybody knows how close you people are. Suppose he, innocently of course, brags about you to them. Is that so hard to imagine? The Childers adore you, Martha. I'm sure they brag about you all the time. How hard could it be for a group like the Skulls to find out all about your movements. We don't even know exactly how many of them there are, or even *who* many of them are. That's what secret is all about. And the Illuminati invented secret, the kind of paranoid secret these people practice."

Martha and Sam just sat there and let Matt's words sink in. They both realized that what Matt had said was highly plausible. Martha's rage had been diffused.

"I'm sorry, Matt," she said. "What you say makes a lot of sense. If it is true, Peter will never forgive himself; he is such a love. We are like family. He would be inconsolable. I really hope you are wrong, for Peter's sake. Sam, what are your thoughts?"

"I think it's time to have a meeting with Whitney Broome, the new advisor to the Skulls, as soon as possible. I got his number from Arlen. I'll give him a call later."

The waitress brought out the freshly-roasted, brewed coffee. It was everything Matt said about it and more. Sam didn't say a word. He just closed his eyes and savored the fresh aroma

"They deliver?" he said. That produced a burst of laughter from all three.

CHAPTER TWENTY-ONE

Three days had passed and the children were getting used to having guards accompany them to school. Martha resumed her class schedule, unaware that Arlen had her and the school under surveillance. Each new day made Sam more apprehensive. Sam knew that if someone was determined to harm his family, they probably would, at all costs. Meanwhile, Injun Jim had taken up his position as Aunt Clara's constant companion. There wasn't a comedy team on the radio that could rival these two. They were a comedy match, made in heaven. Aunt Clara had a comment to make no matter what the poor fellow did. As strange as it may seem, they would be lost without each other. It was not a love affair; it was simply love. At this time in their lives they were exactly what each other needed—companionship and devotion.

The telephone was ringing as Sam came through the door to Aunt Clara's. Mary answered it and handed it to her father. "It's for you, Daddy, from South Carolina," she said.

Sam took the call from Chief White, down in Columbia. He listened intently as Chief White related some very important news. Finally, the chief signed off and Sam joined the family at the dinner table in Aunt Clara's dining room. Everyone wanted to hear the news. Sam decided that this was one time when the children did not have to leave the room, but hear some good news concerning Cousin Caroline.

"Chief White got a visit from one of Caroline's friends, a co-worker at the Bureau. She told the chief that Caroline had met Kempler at a town picnic. She said Caroline felt sorry for the man as he had no money and no place to live. He claimed he was on his way to Florida, and was looking for honest work. They started dating, as Caroline was lonely; and she had a reputation for helping people in need. The woman became suspicious when Caroline told her that she was literally supporting the man. He got a job in a local mill, but never seemed to have any money. The woman could see that Caroline was drawn to the man, but her friend began to become alarmed when Caroline was investing so much into a relationship with a man of questionable character. But Caroline seemed to really enjoy the relationship, so her friend tried to accept it. When Caroline disappeared, the woman was sure that Kempler was at the center of whatever was going on.

The police and the FBI have ruled out any criminal activity where Caroline was concerned. They could not find one piece of evidence of any wrongdoing on her part. After investigating everything possible, they found that Kempler had no contact whatsoever with anyone else in Columbia. It also appears that he made no phone calls and gave the impression that he wanted no contact with anyone except Caroline. Evidently, he realized it would only be a matter of time before he would be found and dealt with, while probably becoming very fond of Caroline. She had that kind of effect on people. The chief felt that Kempler probably never suspected whoever killed him would kill her also. The chief had no knowledge of the murder of the woman at Bayview.

There was one more piece of information. At least three people, including a train conductor for the railroad, were sure they recognized Dieter. He rented a room at a local hostel, but only stayed three days. It was exactly at the time of the murders. One more thing—it would be impossible for anyone to have any German associations down there and go undetected. Columbia is pure south, and *all* American. He was glad to be able to put our family at ease. Caroline was completely exonerated. The Bureau is placing her name on their Wall of Remembrance. That pretty much does it for them. The chief is sure that the solving of this case is going to happen up here. I sure hope he is right. Aunt Clara, that means we can take Caroline home as soon as possible."

Aunt Clara said nothing, but got up from her chair and walked over to hug her nephew. Sam could see the tears in her eyes.

"Thank the Lord for that," she said. "And thank you, Sam."

She turned and headed for the kitchen. It was time for dinner.

CHAPTER TWENTY-TWO

At Sunday service, Pastor Linus Foster reminded the congregation about the newspaper, rubber and metal drives being conducted locally, to help the war effort. The children had been collecting old newspapers for weeks. As soon as the family got home from church, the children changed into their play clothes and started to bring all the papers they had collected up from Aunt Clara's cellar.

Martha was sitting at the kitchen table savoring her first after-service cup of coffee. She was lost in her thoughts of the confrontation with a very bold man at the Yale library. Mary placed a small stack of papers on the kitchen table. Martha only half-consciously glanced down at the picture on the front page. Suddenly, she grew pale, as if she had seen a ghost.

"Sam, Sam," she shouted. "Oh my goodness. I can't believe this."

Sam came running in from his comfortable seat on Aunt Clara's front porch overlooking Wolf Harbor. "What is it?" he said.

Martha did not answer, but pointed down to a man's picture.

"That's the man from the library."

"Are you sure?" Sam asked.

"Believe me," said Martha, "that is one face I will not soon forget. But what is he doing with Mayor Tinsley?"

"Good question," said Sam. "But part of this picture is missing."

"Let me take a look-see," said Aunt Clara. "This picture was taken at the Memorial Day celebration up at the town green. I remember that man. He and another man spent a lot of time in the mayor's company. No one could quite figure out who they were. This being an election year, most folks figured they were money people who came out to contribute to his campaign. Lots of people who come to live here keep to themselves. Folks come here for privacy, and we sure have plenty of that to go around. Besides, many of the people who live up river seldom venture down here.

Sam was quiet. Not what Martha or Aunt Clara expected.

"Not again," said Sam, finally. "Didn't we just go through this with him?"

Without waiting for a response, Sam said, "The mayor is a blowhard, not a traitor. Questioning him is going to start a real circus around here. I don't see that I have much of a choice. I'll have to bring him in for questioning. I can't wait to see the town's reaction to that. Things are about to get real interesting around here. Hold onto your hats."

Sam got in touch with the mayor and asked him to accompany the two local police officers he was sending to pick him up. The officers were under orders to bring the mayor to the local police station for questioning. The mayor obliged, but he was not too happy about it. It was Sunday, and the mayor was spending a restful day at home.

"What's this all about, Sam?" said the mayor.

Sam showed him the picture of the man in the photograph. The caption underneath identified the man as Wilhelm Dieter. The mayor looked puzzled.

"Who is he?" Sam said.

"Darned if I know," said the mayor. "He and some other fellow were very interested in Charles Island, down in Milford."

"What, in particular?" Sam said.

"What else?" said the mayor, "Captain Kidd's treasure. Must have asked me a hundred questions. Said they were sent by some historical society to see if the treasure was for real."

"Why ask you?" Sam asked.

"I'll tell you why. Somehow they found out that one of my hobbies is pirates' treasures. I have an extensive collection of material on famous pirates and their treasures."

"Did they have any credentials?" Sam asked. The mayor grew quiet. "It was a holiday, Sam, for goodness sakes. I was just trying to enjoy the festivities and talk to as many people as I could. It never dawned on me to ask for any credentials."

Sam said nothing, but the mayor knew exactly what he was thinking. The mayor was not feeling so good. "Why do you want to know about this guy, Sam?" he asked.

"The man in the picture is a prime suspect and is wanted for questioning in four murders, one being that of my cousin Caroline, down in South Carolina," said Sam. "And one, a US Naval Intelligence officer."

The mayor's body grew tense. "Oh my," was all he could say. But he started to take on the appearance of someone who was really getting nervous. "I swear to you Sam, I don't know him. Who else is he suspected of killing?"

"His partner, and a lady who was a regular customer at a bar in Milford," said Sam. "I'm very sorry, Mayor, but I now have to list you as a person with possible connections to Nazi spies."

"You can't be serious," said the mayor, jumping up from his seat. "Nazi spies! You honestly believe I could be involved with Nazis?" he protested.

"Maybe not willingly, or even knowingly, but I have to make absolutely sure that your contact with them was a one-time occurrence. The State Department and the U.S. Navy have placed me in charge of the investigation locally, and you stand a better chance with me than with them. I'm sure they will not go gently on anyone they feel is a suspect. I can tell you that the Navy is just looking for a chance to join in, here. From what I have seen, they are not too excited at being left out, especially since they are so close by."

"This is an election year, Sam. The closer we get to October, the worse this is going to be for me. I absolutely have no involvement with any Nazis, period. I will cooperate in any way that I can," said the mayor. "You have to clear me, Sam. Please, how can I look my neighbors in the eye if they suspect me of being a traitor?"

"I need to be able to search your home and office right now. Do I have your permission to do that?" Sam said.

The mayor did not answer immediately. His mind had wandered off.

"Sir, I need to do this. Will I have to get a court order or will you allow me access?" Sam asked.

"Yes, yes of course," said the Mayor, finally. "Do whatever you need to do." The mayor was having a difficult time focusing.

"I'm going to keep you here for the time being. I'll complete my search as quickly as I can," said Sam, who gave instructions to the local police, then with the keys to the mayor's home and office in hand, departed. Sam called

Martha to join him. Martha had proven invaluable in his last investigation, and, being that it was a Sunday and most of his off-duty people were probably off enjoying the weather, he thought her participation could be helpful. The war had depleted the civil forces and the lines were pretty thin. And honestly, Sam was feeling pretty confident that in all likelihood, there would be nothing incriminating to find anyway.

❋   ❋   ❋

Sam rang the doorbell to the mayor's home in the prestigious Champlin Square. When no one answered, he used the key to gain entry. The mayor's home was large and very impressive. Every piece of furniture looked like a collector's item; things one would find in the finest galleries. The mayor was from old money, and lots of it.

Sam took the downstairs where the mayor had a library, office, and drawing room, while Martha took the living quarters upstairs. Sam planned to tackle the library, with its vast number of books last, if they found nothing else. After an hour or so, Sam heard Martha calling from the landing at the top of the stairs. He made his way up the stairs and followed her to the mayor's bedroom. The nightstand next to the mayor's bed had a faux wall in the drawer. Martha realized that this drawer was not as deep as the one on the other side of the bed.

Sam pulled the drawer out and worked the back wall gently loose. There were four letters addressed to the mayor from Dieter. Each one outlined Dieter's plans, and the actions he had to take. Each letter intimated that the mayor was a go-between to report to his superiors, who were close by.

Sam was stunned by the revelation. He and Martha took another hour to go through all the books to the library. They found nothing new.

Sam closed up the house and proceeded with Martha to the mayor's office. Instead of feeling elated, he found he was sad. Martha gave him plenty of space. She left him alone to his thoughts.

The mayor's office stood to be an easier task. And sure enough, they found three more letters from Dieter. Each letter explained in detail Dieter's actions and the events that dictated his actions. In each letter, he expressed his remorse for being forced to take such drastic actions. Sam's sadness was giving way to anger. He and Martha headed back. Sam dropped her off at the house and proceeded to the town police station.

Sam walked into the station and asked one of the officers to accompany him to the Mayor's cell.

"Cuff him," said Sam to the policeman and a greatly confused mayor.

Before the mayor could speak, Sam informed him, "Mayor, I am placing you under arrest for suspicion of treasonous and criminal activities. You will be incarcerated in New Haven. We do not need to incite any violent reactions from the local people. That would cause us problems. You may contact your attorney, once you are booked. I advise you not to say anything, Sir. I would be duty-bound to use anything you say in your prosecution."

The look of disbelief and hurt in the mayor's eyes was something Sam took notice of. Somewhere in the back of his mind, he had a nagging feeling that the mayor was being set up. But by whom, and why? This case was getting stranger by the minute, and Sam was becoming more and more frustrated. Like it or not, Sam was really beginning to entertain the idea of Martha taking a much larger presence in his investigation.

Sam really had read her books. They were a welcome relief from the concerns of the war and from the daily pressures of raising three very bright young children on his own. The size of his jurisdiction seemed twice as large, with a force that was half its normal size. Martha's stories were told with a sense of humor. Her imagination was something that Sam really enjoyed. He especially marveled at her faithful use of police procedures, to weave her tales of investigation and capture. And more than once, Sam had wondered just what this Martha Frost person would really be like. Now that he knew, first-hand, he welcomed her wild imagination for scenarios and motivations, to contribute ideas for Sam's consideration. As far as Sam was concerned, nothing Martha could dream up could be more puzzling or bizarre than this case. A week had gone by, and there were no new sightings of Dieter since the library incident. Sam was beginning to get that feeling in his gut that Dieter was long gone.

Sam had called Matt D'Onofrio, down in New Haven, to clear the way for the mayor to be jailed there, away from Essex. He had cleared it with the governor, who was starting to feel pressure from the state department. Sam's next move would be to try to set up a meeting with the Skulls, and do it as soon as possible.

CHAPTER TWENTY-THREE

Sam was sitting in his office, just staring out into space. He had just gotten off the phone with State's Attorney Jefferson Fine's office, informing him that he was to drop everything and come up to Hartford for a meeting with Fine and the governor, at the State house. Ezra Tinsley's presence in the mix was stirring troubled waters.

As if Sam needed any other surprises, his reverie was broken by the sound of his sergeant's voice informing him that he had a visitor. Sam told the sergeant to bring the person in. Sam rose to his feet to welcome an impeccably dressed man in his mid-thirties.

"Good morning, Captain, I am Whitney Broome. I believe you wanted to see me."

Sam took the man's hand and said, "Yes, I do, but I did not intend to inconvenience you. I would have gladly come down to New Haven."

"Not a problem," said Broome. "As a matter of fact, I would prefer to get as far away from Yale as I can. No need to subject my group to any more scrutiny, given the events of July. I'm sure that any meeting we could have in New Haven, would only lead to more wild speculation. Our people come from the finest families. No need to subject them to any unfavorable publicity."

Sam just smiled and bade Broome take a seat. After Broome refused any refreshments, he and Sam sat down to business.

"Just what is it that makes you feel that you need to speak to me? Have you found any evidence leading back towards Yale?" he wanted to know.

"I have been told that the Skull and Bones has had close ties with the Illuminati over the years. As that group is part of our investigation, I need to know if your people are in any way connected to them," said Sam.

"You know, of course, that organization has been extinct for almost 200 years. How on earth could we possibly have any relationship with a non-existent group?" Broome said.

Sam did not answer. He just leaned back in his chair.

"Okay, Captain, let's put our cards on the table," said Broome. "You have Ivy League written all over you, Captain. I have taken the liberty to gain some knowledge of the man who was going to question me. I know how you brought down Arrington and his band of traitors. I also know that with your family and breeding, you could have done just about anything you set your sights on. You chose family and public service. I greatly admire and respect that. I have also been told that you are a fair man. And, that you have a very powerful ally. So I will save you a lot of time and wasted energy, Sir. The Skulls have nothing to do with the case you are investigating. We are patriots and the families we represent are a cross-section of the finest this country has to offer.

Investigate all you like. But be advised, any attempts by anyone to bring us into this mess with the express purpose to use us or damage us, or our reputation, will be met with the full weight of all that we have at our disposal. We prefer to live in the shadows. There is no need for us to be exposed to the light of day. The press would just love that. I give you my word, Captain, that we will cooperate totally, should there be any real reason to suspect us."

"You're right when you say I am a public servant. I take that responsibility very seriously. I have no intention of involving your group. There is an enormous amount of pressure coming down from the White House over this case. National security seems to be at stake here. I give you my word that I will treat your organization fairly. But I promise you, if I find out that you have withheld information from me, or that you are giving aid to someone who was involved, you will need the help of every one of those families."

Now it was Broome's turn to be silent and offer a smile. It was obvious that both men knew exactly where the other stood. Sam stood up. This meeting was over.

"It was a pleasure to meet you, Captain" said Broome. "I have every confidence that our business is concluded."

"I hope so," said Sam. "You have a very powerful group, Sir. There is no end to what you might learn if you really wanted to. I would be very grateful for any help you might be able to offer. No one needs to know where it came from."

The two men shook hands, and Broome turned and took his leave. His driver opened the rear door of the large black Chrysler sedan, and Broome got in. He never looked back as the expensive vehicle pulled away.

Sam had only one thought on his mind at the moment. "It seems that a lot of people are investigating me."

CHAPTER TWENTY-FOUR

Sam pulled into a parking spot at the State Capitol, marked *Official State Vehicles Only*. He was right on time for his 3PM meeting with the Governor and State's Attorney Fine. The ride to Hartford had not been a pleasant one. This was not the first case Sam had seen where nothing seemed to be going right for his investigation, but the threat to his own family, and a case where national security really was at stake, were weighing heavily on him. How desperate were these people? He needed to know. And just how committed were they to do harm to his family? Sam needed some real help, and none seemed to be making an appearance. He was not looking forward to this meeting with the governor.

Sam entered the main doors to the State House, and was immediately escorted to the governor's office. That alerted him to the state of urgency that was being held at the Capitol. The Governor greeted him with a warm smile. Fine's smile was much more strained. Sam accepted an offering of coffee. It was times like this when he wished he were a drinking man. He was sure that a good stiff drink could make meetings like this one more tolerable. Sam knew the territory well. The Governor was a politician first, and a public servant second, third or fourth; that was anybody's guess. Fine, on the other hand, was a different story. Sam didn't like him. In fact, he didn't like anything about him. Fine was all about power, and he used the law and his office to wield that power. As far as Sam was concerned, neither of these men shared any concerns for those whom they swore to serve. Whatever their agenda was, it all boiled down to protecting their own interests. The President of the United States was watching very closely. These guys were under a lot of heat.

"How plausible is Tinsley's possible involvement in all this?" asked the Governor, not wasting any time with formalities.

"Right now, very," said Sam.

"Care to elaborate?" asked Fine.

"I have seven letters addressed to him by a man named Wilhelm Dieter, a Nazi spy who has admitted to committing four murders, including that of a US Naval Intelligence officer. I found these letters in his home and in his office. They were obtained with his full permission, witnessed by two police officers in Essex."

"But there is a problem?" Fine questioned.

Sam took a moment to answer. "Tinsley is a blowhard. I've known him most of my life. Our families were once very close. His parents and mine did business together. The man just does not have the intestinal fortitude to be a part of something this big. He was not a bit nervous when I brought him in for questioning. And this man worries about everything. Yet, when I brought him in, he was very composed; confused, but composed. These are not the actions of a man like Mayor Tinsley. We have to go on what is staring us in the face, but something just doesn't seem right."

"Maybe you are conflicted where his family is concerned," said Fine.

Sam looked at Fine with questioning eyes. "Conflicted?" he said.

"Some people have told us that there is a history between you and his daughter," said Fine.

"With Allison?" said Sam. "Where are these people from, Idaho? The only history Allison Tinsley and I share is that we live in the same town and that her father is our Mayor. I don't know what you are trying to prove here, but these kinds of accusations, or reckless insinuations are not very wise when they have no basis in truth. If you are trying to get a rise out of me you're wasting all our time."

"Tell us about the Illuminati, and where you think they fit into this case," said Fine, without responding to Sam's answer.

Sam sat back in his chair and stifled a laugh. "The only way you could have known about that is to have spoken to Whitney Broome. I made sure not to mention that to anyone else. I'll make note of the fact that you are an acquaintance of a person of interest in this case. I'll be sure to relay that bit of information to the State Department in my report," said Sam.

"I told you he was good," said the Governor, looking in Fine's direction.

Now it was Fine's turn to take a moment. "I'm sorry to put you through this, Captain, but we are under enormous pressure here. The President's people have convinced him that Bridgeport would be a prime target for mass destruction. The military is always paranoid, but the Governor and I have to admit that that is a real possibility. This Dieter fellow has been pretty ruthless. There seems to be nothing he won't do to achieve his objectives, whatever they are. Tell us, what have you come up with?"

Sam decided to share a scenario that Martha had suggested. Admittedly, it was wild, but it sure was a possibility.

"It's possible that the Nazis are interested in two things: crippling our war machinery in Bridgeport, and finding Captain Kidd's treasure on Charles Island in Milford. A group of Bavarian monks might have found the treasure. They gave every indication that they were sympathetic to the German cause. It has been discovered that they took gold back to Bavaria, where they could have convinced the Nazis concerning the treasure's authenticity. This is a wild idea, I must admit, but if the Nazis were to bomb that large storage tank in Bridgeport, it would be devastating to the area. The whole area would be impacted, and every available police, fire and emergency unit would spring into action. While achieving their objective to destroy our factories, they would also gain a great advantage towards extracting the treasure without fear of detection or interference. I'm sure the Navy unit at the Villa Rosa in Woodmont, would not be paying too much attention to the Charles Island area. That would be some coup if they could pull it off."

The Governor and Fine sat in stunned silence.

"This Dieter character has impressed me that if, in fact, this was his real purpose for coming here, he would be just bold enough to go it alone. I'm sure he would even be willing to die for his cause.

I sincerely hope there is no one here to give him a hand. Meanwhile, he seems to have vanished," said Sam.

"What can I do?" the Governor asked.

"I suggest you get in touch with the Superintendant of the Bridgeport Police Department as soon as possible, and tell him to discreetly use his harbor patrol to take up a 24-hour surveillance of the harbor, especially where that huge tank is. There is a large hotel in the vicinity. It would be wise to place police up on the roof to keep watch over the area facing away from the harbor. Make sure every guard in the factories in the near vicinity of that tank, keeps his eyes peeled. Tell them this is no time to relax. Dieter is ruthless. The man has killed four people that we know of, one of whom was his partner. I believe he is capable of anything he feels is necessary to achieve this objective."

The Governor slowly rose to his feet. "I'm glad they chose you, Sam," he said. I will get on the horn to Bridgeport, immediately. If there is anything you need, just call me."

The governor tore a piece of paper from a pad on his desk. He wrote down a phone number.

"This is the number for state emergencies. It is in operation twenty four hours a day, even on holidays. They will know how to reach me, no matter what, no matter when. I appreciate your coming up here on such short notice. Be safe, Captain, and thank you."

Sam shook hands with the Governor and the state's attorney. He made his way back to his vehicle. Martha's scenario made perfect sense. The more Sam thought about it, the more plausible the whole idea seemed. It was obvious that the Governor and Fine thought so. At least now, something was being done. The big question now was, is Dieter gone or was he getting ready to do the things Martha had suggested? Sam had to wonder. Could one man really pull this off? The ride back was no more restful than the one up to Hartford.

❄   ❄   ❄

Three more days had passed, making the number *ten* days, since Martha's encounter with Dieter at the Yale library. By now, the whole town was aware of Mayor Tinsley's arrest, and to no one's surprise, the whole town was talking. Mayor Tinsley's stock was plunging rapidly. The Mayor was right; he knew human nature. It only took a few hours for the people to go from questioning how true the accusations against him were, to brewing a full scale lynch mob mentality. Sam was glad he had made the decision to incarcerate the mayor down in New Haven. Given the nature of the charges, and the gravity of someone being held for possible treason, Sam was absolutely convinced that he had made the right decision. A chance encounter with Allison Tinsley on Main Street, produced a look of pure contempt when their eyes met. Still, Allison said nothing. Sam was grateful, given Allison's ability to become explosive at times. He was holding out hope that the Mayor was innocent.

Everywhere you looked around town, people were gathering to air their opinions. The Black Swan was alive with constant gatherings, especially in the bar area. Wanda had purchased Zuckerman's, and made her brother Louis Peoples a partner in the venture. Peoples took over running the place, and seemed to be doing a good job of it. Of course, the place was now the home away from home for the local elder gents to expound upon their many theories. The children were not allowed there without supervision. The talk could get pretty heated. The Peterson Brothers' garage was also experiencing an increase in local gatherings. The whole town was abuzz, and the buzz was not going well for Mayor Tinsley. And still, no sign of Dieter.

Meanwhile Aunt Clara was putting the finishing touches on her preparations for Caroline Tyler's memorial service, to be held on Saturday. Aunt Clara had decided against taking Caroline's ashes to Pearl Harbor. She made a decision to bury Caroline with her mother. Traveling to Pearl Harbor was simply too great a journey, especially since it would require that Martha go along with her. Sam was relieved that reason had prevailed over emotion. Aunt Clara was at peace with her decision. The Memorial Mass was to be attended only by family and close friends of the Tylers.

※　※　※

Things were too quiet for Sam's liking. Arlen Templeton's men were keeping a constant vigil over the children and Sam kept reminding everyone not to lower their guard. Sam decided to pay Arlen another visit; he felt a new perspective on the course of the war might shed some light on actions, or recent lack of actions by the Nazis.

As usual, Templeton was waiting in the courtyard as Sam drove up.

"How are things going?" Arlen asked.

"Quiet," said Sam, "too quiet. Things were happening pretty fast and then nothing. What I need to know is if these people are gone or just reloading."

"The war isn't going quite the way Hitler envisioned it," said Arlen. "There is a lot of unrest in Germany. Hitler seems to be taking more and more control of the military, and the word is there is trouble in paradise. There is talk that Rommel has fallen out of favor, and there are rumors suggesting some of Hitler's top military minds are trying to kill him. Hitler rarely appears out in public anymore for fear of his life. The more he takes control of the military strategy, the more he incurs the wrath of his generals. The man has no military experience and seems to be acting totally on impulse. It sounds as though he's quite delusional. The Russians are giving the Germans quite a tough go of it in Stalingrad. It is starting to look as though Japan is fighting with more resolve. The Germans have been seduced by Hitler, but now that things aren't going so well for the Fatherland, the people are beginning to fear the worst. The Japanese will fight to the bitter end. That's all they know. They are no strangers to war. They have been warring for centuries. Their resolve will prove much greater in the long run."

Sam listened intently to what Arlen had to say. By now, he knew not to ask how Arlen knew so much. He had learned to take Arlen at his word; he had no reason to doubt any of it.

"If what you are saying is true, it stands to reason that a strike on American soil, especially Bridgeport, would be a great morale booster for Hitler. And if the Bavarians really have located a treasure, that money would work greatly in his favor," said Sam.

Arlen quickly interjected, "Hitler is running out of finances and resources. He was counting on taking the resources of fallen nations. That just has not happened. His losses in equipment and lives have been staggering. I'm sure he's getting panicky. England has valiantly repelled him; France has fallen, but the resistance has caused him nothing but headaches. Fighting in Russia is no picnic. Northern Africa is just about ours and Patton has no one left to stop him. Be very careful, Son, these people are desperate, and desperate people of the most dangerous kind."

Sam thanked Arlen and returned home in time to see Injun Jim giving the children a history lesson on Milford, while treating them to a spellbinding tale of pirates, treasures of gold and one Captain Kidd.

CHAPTER TWENTY-FIVE

For most people, Labor Day marks the end of summer. Schools open and the new school year begins. People who live at the shore know that summer weather usually continues through late September, and they hang on to every warm sun-filled day with both hands.

On a day filled with the bluest of skies and gentle warm breezes blowing, Caroline Tyler's ashes were laid to rest alongside her mother in Riverview Cemetery, up on North Main Street. It was a sad day for the Tylers. Caroline's future shined as brightly as a noonday sun in mid-July. Great things were expected of her. It was a foregone conclusion that she would be a great lawyer, one who would possibly sit on the bench of the highest court. Such was her remarkable mind. And now, all that was left for Caroline was the sadness of her family, and the giant unfulfilled future of amazing promise.

It was Sam who had the hardest time wiping away the tears that would not cease flowing. The memory of his little cousin whom he would tease ceaselessly and for whom he filled the role of big brother was making it hard for him to concentrate on anything else. Martha was surprised at Cousin Ellen's tears. She was the eldest of the three, but like Sam, took such joy in Caroline. Sam had once remarked that Lilith seemed to be

Caroline all over again. Even Caroline saw that. She loved to play with Sam's three children on her infrequent visits. Moving to South Carolina was to be a short intermission, before she came back home to resume her career in Boston. Sadly, it was, but just not the return everyone expected. Even Judge Romney Baines, of the Boston Circuit Court, was in attendance.

It was he who had seen Caroline's promise at Harvard Law, and who had a job waiting for her when she returned. The sadness in his eyes was not lost on Martha.

Once again, Aunt Clara's lawn was the place for a reception. Injun Jim had not yet returned the tents to his Gypsy friends, and the largest provided shade and setting for the forty people in attendance. Wanda Loomis supplied the food, and the Templetons supplied the tables, chairs and everything else necessary for the catering. There were so many warm memories of such a beautiful young life, so terribly shortened by a seemingly ruthless act of violence.

Sam came walking across the lawn to rejoin Martha. He had gotten away for a while to clear his mind and had a surprise for Martha.

"I just put in a call to Perkins down in Milford," he said, in answer to her questioning his absence. "Aunt Clara and Injun Jim are taking the children up to Hamburg Cove to visit some old friends tomorrow. Arlen's men will be going along. The family will be very safe. So I thought I would take the opportunity to take you on a little journey."

❉   ❉   ❉

Church service got out at 11 AM on Sunday morning, and soon, Aunt Clara and Injun Jim and the children headed out towards Hamburg Cove, with four of Arlen Templeton's security people following two boat lengths behind. Sam loved driving down US #1 through the small towns along the shoreline. He never tired of the clean, crisp air and of the landscape of life so close to the sea.

"I had to do something to get past my thoughts yesterday," he had told Martha. "It occurred to me that you should see Milford. It is such an interesting place, fascinating really. I'm sure that mind of yours will be working overtime once you see all that this little town has to offer. It's really quite unique."

Martha loved the idea and was only too happy to oblige her husband. She was grateful that he was able to overcome his sadness and think of her in the process. She loved being Mrs. Samuel Tyler.

Sam followed Officer Perkins directions and turned left off Route#1 at Naugatuck Avenue, in the Devon section of Milford, then proceeded one and one quarter miles towards the shore. Sam stopped at a red light one block from the end of Naugatuck, and saw Officer Perkin's police vehicle parked on the right-hand side with Perkins leaning against it waiting for Sam's arrival.

"Follow me," the officer instructed.

Perkins got in his vehicle and made a left onto Broadway East. Sam and Martha were surprised to see the streets filled with people who were enjoying a street carnival atmosphere that seemed to go on for quite a distance. On the right-hand side was one game of chance booth after another. On the left there were a few small restaurants and a small amusement park with rides and a large bumping car facility. Sam and Martha were amazed.

Perkins made a right hand turn through a very small opening between two wooden arcade structures that opened to a good size parking lot. There were cottages and rooming houses everywhere. They parked, exited their vehicles and then followed Perkins' lead along the sandy walkway between two cottages.

Then, Sam and Martha stopped dead in their tracks. There, right in front of them, was the land bridge that led to Charles Island, which Perkins had told Sam about. Perkins had a wide grin on his face. Sam looked over at Martha whose eyes were full of wonderment. Sam knew this was going to be a good day.

"We have about two hours before the tide makes walking a little risky," said Perkins.

That said, they made their way along the quarter mile walkway out to Charles Island. The island was not very large, but big enough to house a few decent sized buildings and an outdoor sanctuary. Perkins walked them around the perimeter, then took them into the largest building. It was only about eight hundred square feet in size. It appeared to be a meeting facility with a kitchen. It was a good bet that this is where the Brothers took their meals. Perkins led them to a small stairwell in the back that led down to a cellar that was about the same size as the room above. He led them over to a wall that had a large storage shelving unit attached to it, pressed against it, then stepped back as the wall swung open. Martha let out a gasp. Sam just smiled at her.

"Don't you write about things like this?" Sam kidded her.

"Very funny," said Martha.

"Watch your step," said Perkins. "Remember, we are under sea level and on an island. If I say get back, then get back as fast as you can, no questions. Got it?"

Sam nodded affirmative, then took Martha in tow. He knew there was no way she could be persuaded not to go along. The tunnel was about 75 feet long, with storage rooms off the main hallway. Perkins' assessment was dead on. It appeared that the tunnel was used to access the Prichard estate. Every ten or so feet, there was a sconce on the walls for torches. There was no electricity.

"Somewhere, down here, is another passageway. But no one wants to attempt to find it. If these walls were to go, there is no escape. Nobody seems too anxious to chance it no matter how much gold they say is down here," said Perkins. Sam and Martha went into each storage area but were careful not to touch any of the walls for fear of causing them to collapse.

Once back outside, they took a little more time to walk around. Martha had a pad and pen, and was furiously writing notes. Sam was pleased that she was obviously enjoying herself. Every once in a while she would look over at him and smile. He caught every one.

The group walked back across the land bridge to Myrtle Beach, which was alive with activity.

"These people are going to drain every last drop of summer, you can count on that," said Perkins.

"Who could blame them?" Martha said. "What a wonderful place this is."

"Folks come here from all over; New York mostly," said Perkins. "It's a whole different way of life for them. Milford is real laid-back. People here know how to relax. I guess it just rubs off on the visitors. Some keep coming, right up to October. Once the weather changes, it's just the locals, but you would be surprised how many people that is. Still, it's pretty quiet around here through the winter. But come spring, man, this place really starts to come alive, all the way over to Woodmont."

"We all set, Perkins?" Sam asked.

"Sure enough, Captain," said Perkins.

"What now?" Martha asked.

"Just another little surprise for my fair lady," said Sam.

Once again, they were back in their vehicles. Sam followed Perkins out to the main street and through the back roads, up to the Milford green. It was here that Martha witnessed something she had not seen in a very long time: a police officer directing traffic from an elevated cylindrical station at a four-way intersection, at the north end of the green. He was affectionately known by the children of the town as the policeman in the garbage can.

"Officer Jack," Perkins informed Martha after they exited their vehicles, "a real crowd pleaser hereabouts. The man is a local folk hero."

Sam followed Perkins into the Milford Harbor parking lot, found a parking space, then he and Martha followed Perkins over to the dock. A police launch was waiting, motor running and ready to go. Perkins said a few words to the other officer who would be steering the boat, and joined Martha and Sam on the bow. The launch slowly made its way out of the harbor past a very large number of sailboats.

"Milford is known for its sailboats," said Perkins, as they made their way past the yacht club and out towards Charles Island.

CHAPTER TWENTY-SIX

"Like we planned?" The officer driving the boat asked.

"You betcha'," said Perkins.

"I've seen all this on a map, but there is nothing like experiencing the real thing," said Sam. "Bridgeport is just two towns away, and I wanted to get a real feel for the distance. When I thought about your scenario, it made me wonder just how much of a distance that was. I asked Perkins to take us there and then back, all the way to Woodmont, at the far end of Milford, to get an idea of what the Germans were thinking. Obviously, someone must have done what we are doing now, to give them assurance that such a plan was feasible. Whatever the case, I'm sure that after we get done, we'll have a pretty good idea of how much of this plan, if not all of it, makes sense logistically."

Martha listened intently to all Sam had to say. She did not respond, but began writing more notes to herself.

They set a course southeast, out and around Charles Island, before turning southward towards Bridgeport.

"This is the Housatonic River that separates Milford and Stratford," said Perkins.

Soon they were going along the coast of neighboring Stratford, and its beaches.

"This is Lordship," said Perkins. "It is a very exclusive area of Stratford. Lots of big homes. Very quiet and private. Bridgeport is straight ahead."

It wasn't long before a large amusement park with a very large wooden roller coaster came into view. Two giant signal towers, one at each end of the park, reached up high into the sky.

"Pleasure Beach," said Perkins.

Before they could react to the presence of Pleasure Beach, which sat on an island just off the coast of Bridgeport, they came face to face with the huge storage facility, right there on the harbor. For a moment, Sam and Martha were speechless.

"Holy . . .," was all Martha was able to muster.

"Can you imagine that?" Perkins said. "I'd really like to meet the genius who came up with that idea."

Sam understood fully. Everyone in the greater Bridgeport area was in exactly the same danger as the inhabitants of Bridgeport. If that tank were to blow, there was no telling how much devastation there would be. And really, that tank seemed to be an open invitation for disaster.

"I would never have believed it if I had not seen it for myself," said Sam. "We saw it last week, but that was from land and at quite a distance. This view gives us a whole different perspective. Thank God it hasn't been attacked. Now I know why the governor is so nervous. I don't think the State is prepared for something of this magnitude happening. I'm surprised there isn't more of a military presence; or is there?"

Perkins didn't respond, but pointed to the driver to head further south. Soon they were moving along a 2 mile stretch of beach that was simply breathtaking.

"This is Seaside Park, once the backyard of the great circus man P. T. Barnum. Beautiful, isn't it?"

"Very," said Martha. Sam agreed.

Perkins continued, "What you can't see, folks, is the huge Sikorsky Aircraft factory just behind it; helicopters ready to deploy troops if necessary. And at the other end, back there in Lordship, is the Sikorsky Airport, where fighter planes are hidden in the hangers, but fully ready if needed. Out past New Haven, is Tweed Airport. Fighter planes there, too. The area is not as vulnerable as you might think. But if that tank is hit, well, I don't know how much help any of them would be."

Through it all, Martha was filling her pad with notes. Sam motioned for Perkins to turn around and head back to Milford. The sight of Charles Island was a welcome relief. The driver headed out towards Long Island, and made a course towards West Haven, the town that bordered Milford on the water. Then they came about and moved closer to the shore, in a southerly direction. Within moments Martha got her first look at the Villa Rosa. By now the tide was up and the underground entrance was accessible. But they would not be going in. Sam had informed Commander Thomas that he and Martha would be in the neighborhood, but would not be stopping by for afternoon tea.

"Oh, Sam, how beautiful," said Martha. "And those homes," she said, pointing to the ten smaller walled estates, sitting behind their private crescent beach. "I'll bet this place was really something when Mister Poli was alive. I wonder how many movie stars and important people came here to visit."

"Lots of important people from all walks of life came here in Poli's hey-day," said Perkins. Clarke Gable, Francis Langford, the Duke of Windsor with his questionable lady, to name just a few. Old man Poli had homes set aside for these people. And all were fully staffed. The locals always made sure that their privacy was respected. And, honestly, no one wanted to upset the Poli family. They did so much for the community."

As they moved along, they came face to face with the giant walled community called Morningside, sitting high above sea level. The homes on the natural stone wall, usually 20 to 30 feet high, had a magnificent view of the Poli mansions and the breadth of Long Island Sound. There were few places along the whole coastline of Connecticut to rival it. Sam informed Martha that the hotel at the top was where the naval investigator, Agent Lipton, was murdered.

Soon, they were nearing Bayview, where Mary Lou Donovan had washed up onto shore, and finally they were back at Milford Harbor, and land. Now Sam and Martha had a much clearer perspective of things. The ride back to Essex was filled with the airing of their thoughts and opinions. Of course, their reasons were quite different. Now, Sam could feel the magnitude of the events that took place with a clear-cut reason for belief in the possibility that Martha's proposed plan was more than doable. Martha, on the other hand, was getting dizzy at the thought of a delicious murder mystery she was concocting. How close she would be to the real ending depended heavily on now successful Sam's efforts were.

Suddenly, Martha got quiet. Sam could see that she was deep in thought.

"What's going on in that fertile mind of yours?" Sam asked.

"You were right when you said we should see the coastline. I am as convinced as you, that Charles Island and that monstrosity of a storage tank in Bridgeport, are connected. As I see it, either one of them could be a target, but both would take more than two operatives, no matter how good they are. And now that there is only one, I have the distinct feeling that it would take a team of men to carry out their plans," said Martha.

"And that would mean that this team would have to be close enough to be ready to strike and avoid detection, when they were ready to make their move," said Sam. "I have an idea how that could be accomplished.

"It would be difficult for a group of Germans to go undetected on land for any length of time," said Martha. "They would probably have to be given a specific date, so they could assemble quickly and strike. What are you thinking?"

"A boat," said Sam.

"What kind of boat could go undetected?" Martha asked.

"A very large one. One headed for New Haven Harbor: tankers. They go in and out on a regular basis. They also drop anchor some miles out, to wait for clearance to proceed for docking. It's not unusual for them to stay out on the sound overnight, before coming into port. It wouldn't take much for the Germans to set that up, once the date was established. They could use a launch to easily make it to shore. But they would have to be really organized to strike almost immediately," said Sam.

"Not necessarily," said Martha. "Not if they had somewhere to organize and fine tune their plans, somewhere people don't usually go."

"The tunnels," said Sam. "No one is to go in there without authorization."

They sat in silence for a few moments, gathering their thoughts.

"There is another room," said Sam, emphatically." That is what Dieter found."

"Or the Bavarians," said Martha. "Maybe, they found another room with just enough gold to convince them of the treasure, but just as importantly, a place where someone could stay undetected, maybe not for long, but just long enough to organize, strike, and regroup to make their escape once they were through."

"I like it," said Sam. "I'll notify Commander Thomas at the Villa Rosa, to track every tanker that is scheduled to enter New Haven Harbor. The Germans have relations with Argentina and Venezuela. It wouldn't be too difficult for them to place men on any ship in their registry."

They rode the short distance from Saybrook to home in silence. Sam was beginning to feel tension building within him. He no longer had any doubts that the Germans were going to strike. For the first time, he realized how desperate their plans were, and how much pressure they would be under to succeed. He understood this because he was beginning to experience that same pressure himself. Sam had never had to go to war, and that bothered him. He always felt a hollowness knowing young men were being asked to go far away to a foreign land, and quite possibly lay down their lives there. The thought of that always left him with much sadness. Sure, he had been told by his superiors, how important his work was here. He knew that if war were to come here, he would be expected to play a key role protecting and organizing, on the home front. That never seemed to give him any sense of satisfaction, until now. Now, the war could actually be here, and Sam might be smack in the middle of it. All of a sudden, Sam wasn't feeling very safe; not for himself, his family or his country. It was starting to appear as though the war had come home, and Sam was no longer feeling left out or unduly lucky to be left behind in America. He had often wondered just what he would do if something like this were to happen. It seemed Captain Samuel Tyler of the Connecticut State Police was about to find out.

CHAPTER TWENTY-SEVEN

"What!" yelled Sam, at the news that someone had tried to kill Ezra Tinsley.

Sam was alone in the house. Martha was back at work, and the children were off to school. It was the one morning Sam could relax and take his time going to work. That idea just went up in smoke.

"I haven't even had my first cup of coffee," he said to himself. He grabbed his gun and badge, and headed across the lawn to Aunt Clara's house and hopefully, morning coffee. Ten minutes later he was driving headlong down Route #9 to New Haven, with sirens blasting.

Sam walked into New Haven police headquarters, just in time to see Matt D'Onofrio leading a man in handcuffs towards an interrogation room.

"Tinsley is alright," he was informed by one of the officers. "The sergeant is going to question the man we feel is responsible. He wanted me to tell you that one of the inmates was bullying Tinsley and took his breakfast. He won't be bullying him or anyone else anymore. He died on the way to the hospital. Rat poison in the morning mush they call eggs. Two bites and the tough guy was down for the count. You can go into the observation room. I'll tell the sergeant you are here."

Sam stood in the observation room behind a two-way mirror, as Sergeant D'Onofrio sat across from a young man in his mid-twenties who was already the possessor of a glorious criminal record for one so young.

"We know you did it," said D'Onofrio. "One of your fellow inmates saw you and turned on you to try to make a deal for himself. You should have known that you could not get away with killing someone in jail."

"Wait a minute, wait a minute," yelled the inmate. "I had no idea that stuff was poison. You have to believe me. It was supposed to give him diarrhea and severe stomach pains. They gave me $100 to do it. You think I'm going to kill someone for $100? Rob someone, yeah, but kill them? They said they were really angry at him and wanted to teach him a lesson."

"Who is 'they'?" D'Onofrio asked.

"That crazy group over at Yale," said the inmate. "This guy said he represented them."

"Describe this guy for me," said D'Onofrio.

"Mid-thirties, light hair, you know, with that stupid Ivy League, close-to-the-head look. He was tall and thin, and wore a very expensive suit and shoes. This man was no professor. The clothes were too expensive. The guy definitely was a businessman."

Immediately, Sam and D'Onofrio came to the same conclusion—Whitney Broome.

"Wait here," said D'Onofrio, as he got up to join Sam.

"I can bring Broome in if you want, Sam," said D'Onofrio. "We can both interrogate him."

Sam thought for a moment. "I think I'll try to get Broome to come in on his own. I believe he has ties to the governor, or at least the State's attorney.

We'll need to walk a fine line here. This guy has powerful connections. One thing is for sure, the Skull and Bones have plenty of money to finance an operation of this magnitude. I just find it hard to believe Broome could be so blatant as to meet with this guy openly."

"Yeah, I know what you mean," said D'Onofrio, "but let's not forget how arrogant these people are. I deal with them all the time. They really are full of themselves."

"Money and power have a way of doing that," said Sam. "We know that the Skulls have a German origin, and the Illuminati is Bavarian, and as close to German as you can get without actually being from there. Let me talk to Broome and try to get him to come in on his own. If he is not guilty, he should have no objections. And besides, if he indeed, is not guilty, I'm confident that he would dedicate his life to make yours a living hell for embarrassing him. You guys are right around the corner. It would be no sweat off his brow to make you pay for any discomfort he or his organization might be made to feel."

"Yeah, I get your point," said D'Onofrio. "How does this sound? I have two squad cars in the area to supply backup. If I don't get a call from you within a half-hour, they're moving in."

"Sounds good. As soon as I contact Broome and set up a meeting, I'll call you," said Sam.

Sam put in a call to Broome's office and learned that he was in Hartford for the remainder of the day, and would be back in his office tomorrow morning. Sam insisted that Broome meet him first thing in the morning. He would have to wait for Broome to contact his office. Sam was sure that the attack on Tinsley was a clear indication that whatever the Germans had planned was going to happen very soon. Time was running out. Sam was convinced that the attack on the Mayor was the beginning signal for whatever the Germans were cooking up.

Sam went over to Albertus Magnus to see Martha, to fill her in on Tinsley's narrow escape and the possibility that big things were about to take place. He was greeted by Templeton's men. Seeing them helped put him at ease. Sam and Martha had lunch in the cafeteria. Martha grew uneasy as the conversation made her aware of the dangerous events that were likely to have already been set in motion. It was obvious that this was no Martha Frost drama. It was the real thing, and Sam was going to be right at the center of it. She found herself squeezing his hands very tightly.

"I'm going over to Milford, to meet up with Commander Thomas at the Villa Rosa, to see how we can coordinate everyone involved. Time is short. The best chance we have is to get everyone on the same page as soon as we possibly can. I'll see you for dinner. Aunt Clara and Injun Jim are cooking out. I'll be home around 6. Don't worry, I'm sure Dieter and his people feel very confident right now. Once I find out where Broome stands in all of this, I'll be ready to put the plan into action." They kissed and Sam headed for Milford.

CHAPTER TWENTY-EIGHT

It was 7 AM, and Sam was heading down to New Haven, for an 8 o'clock meeting with Whitney Broome, at Sherman's on the Green. Martha was going to spend the morning at the Saybrook *Sentinel.* In conversation with Aunt Clara during last night's supper, Aunt Clara had made the comment to Martha that she was only seeing half the picture when referring to a local Essex tradition. It was Mary who chimed in and said, "Yes, like that photo in the newspaper I put on Aunt Clara's table."

Sam and Martha looked at each other as if hit with a bolt of lightning.

"We never found out who else was in that picture," said Sam.

"Yes," said Martha, "and it might not be a bad idea for me to go over to the local newspaper office, and look through their files to get a whole copy of that photo. I can't believe we never thought of it."

"Well, we have now," said Sam, knowing he had to act fast. He got in touch with Arlen, to have one of Arlen's men come early that morning to take Martha to the Saybrook *Sentinal.*

❋   ❋   ❋

Sam joined Broome at his table at Sherman's on the Green. Both men ordered coffee.

"I have something serious to discuss with you, so you may not want to order breakfast, or at least not breakfast with me," said Sam.

"It's early and I'm guessing that you have not had anything to eat, Captain. You just came a long way to meet me. I assumed that it was important, and I assure you that I am pretty confident that nothing you say will make me want to skip breakfast. So let's order and then you can fire away."

They ordered and Sam began. "There was an attempt on Ezra Tinsley's life yesterday in jail. Fortunately for him, someone else ate his breakfast that was filled with rat poison. The man died rather quickly. We have the man in custody who put the poison in his food. That man insists he thought he was party to a prank by someone who was upset by Tinsley's actions, and just wanted him to suffer a little. The man described as the one to have put him up to it, and who paid him $100 for his troubles, sounds very much like you."

Broome was buttering his toast, and never stopped or missed a stroke. He just looked up at Sam and said, "What do you think, Captain? Do you believe I could do such a thing? Wait, let me ask you this, now that I think of it. The man who did this is an inmate, yes?"

Sam nodded yes.

"So, if I were to be the one to do this, I would have had to go into the jail to see him, right?"

Again, Sam nodded affirmatively.

"So, it would follow that to do that, I would have to be one of the most arrogant or stupid people under the sun. Is that how you see me?" Before Sam could answer, Broome said, "Let's skip that question, shall we? I suggest we eat our breakfast, and then you can tell me what it is you would like me to do," said Broome.

Sam had to admit that Broome was very self-assured. He just found it hard to believe that Broome was that arrogant or stupid. Finding Broome guilty sure would make his life easier. But something told him that it wasn't going to be that easy. What a neat little package that would be: a powerful secret organization with tons of money, influence, and possible ties to the Illuminati. It was all too simple. But Sam could dream, couldn't he?

"I'd like you to come to the New Haven Police Department, at noon today," said Sam. "I would advise you to bring your attorney. I am sworn to protect the innocent. If you are innocent, Sir, I promise you that I will do my very best to protect you. I believe that something very bad is about to happen, and I don't need to be going on any wild goose chases. Believe it or not, it's going to take a lot of proof to convince me of any wrongdoing on your part."

Broome just sat there for a moment before responding. "You know very well that I have done my research on you, Captain. I will meet you there at noon. I do believe you would be fair, and as such, I find that I trust you. I have read nothing to convince me of anything to the contrary. I hope you enjoyed your breakfast. I will see you at noon."

Sam took the hint. Broome put his napkin down, but did not get up. It was a sign that their business was completed, for the time being at least, and that it was time for Sam to take his leave. As Sam exited the restaurant he had to smile to himself. Truly, Broome was the essence of arrogance.

CHAPTER TWENTY-NINE

Sam pulled into a parking space at the New Haven Police Department. It was 11:45. As he was about to exit his vehicle, he received a call from the barracks.

"Your wife is trying to reach you, Sir," said the desk sergeant "Can I patch her through?"

"Go ahead, Sergeant," said Sam.

"What's up, honey?" Sam asked. "Did you find anything?"

"Boy, did I," said Martha. "You'll never guess who was in that picture with Tinsley and Dieter."

Sam took a moment, then responded, "Lawrence Mulcahy?"

"How on earth did you guess that?" Martha asked.

"It was a wild guess, I'll admit. Actually, it was so ridiculous that it made sense. Mulcahy's name just popped into my head. Let's face it, there aren't too many other possibilities. I'm going in to see Matt and Whitney Broome. I've got something I want you to do," said Sam.

"I've already begun to look into the Mulcahy family," said Martha. "The minute I saw his picture, I knew he was involved in all this. He might just be the mastermind. I have a friend at the *Boston Globe*, and Peter Childers has friends at Harvard. It will take a few hours, but I'm pretty sure we can find out a few things about this Lawrence Mulcahy fellow."

Sam just smiled. "Glad you're on my side, Lady," he said. "I'll be waiting for your call."

All of a sudden, Sam was pretty sure he knew how this session with Broome and the inmate was going to go. Matt D'Onofrio had rounded up four successful local businessmen to assist in a lineup. When he told them the reason for it and of the possible danger on American soil, they were only too happy to oblige. All knew Broome.

Sam and Matt went into the observation room, and had the five businessmen line up in the room behind the glass.

"Take your time," said Matt.

"Is this a joke?" the inmate asked.

"What do you mean?" D'Onofrio asked.

"I told you this guy was a big shot with the Skulls. That should have made it easy for you," said the inmate.

"Are you saying he's not one of these men? None of these men approached you?" Matt asked.

"I've never seen any of these guys. What's going on here?" he asked.

"It appears you have been duped more than once," said Sam. The inmate was now staring at him in disbelief.

"You gotta believe me," he said. "You can't let me take the fall for this. This is murder, and I ain't no murderer. You've got to help me. I've been suckered."

"Relax," said Sam. "We believe you. This whole thing is starting to make sense. I know exactly what happened, and you are right, you have been used by some very resourceful and dangerous people. Send him back to his cell, Matt, and I'll fill you in."

"I'm going to be okay?" the inmate wanted to know.

"If he says you're clean, then you're clean," said Matt to a very relieved inmate.

❋   ❋   ❋

Sam and Matt went over to Willoughby's on Chapel, to get some strong Jamaican brew. Sam filled him in on everything. It was only a matter of time before Martha could gather enough information on Mulcahy to see just how deeply he was involved in all this. Sam was convinced that the Germans were going to strike soon; he just didn't have a timeline down.

"I believe I can help you with that," said D'Onofrio.

Sam looked up from his coffee. The look said, "Well?"

"The vice president will be in Bridgeport tomorrow, to speak at a luncheon to be given in the ballroom of the Stratfield Arms Hotel.

"The Vice President of the United States?" Sam asked, hardly able to believe what he was hearing.

Matt just smiled and forged ahead. "Every major business leader, and all the heads of the local manufacturing facilities will be in attendance. The hotel is less than a quarter-mile from that tank. The Germans won't be acting in daylight, so it has to be tonight. They'll probably set the explosives and then detonate them by radio signal from a safe distance. Whatever you've got planned, my friend, you better set it in motion right away."

Sam and Matt rushed back to the New Haven Police Department. Sam had some calls to make. The first thing he did was to put in a call to the

Villa Rosa command post, and set up a 3 PM meeting with Commander Thomas. Next, he called Milford police and had Bill Perkins inform his chief that Perkins and the police launch would be needed. Sam also called the superintendent of police at Bridgeport, and had him send the police and fire chiefs out to the meeting. His adrenaline was kicking in, on all cylinders. Sam had to calm himself down so as not to get everyone else too excited. Cool heads were going to be necessary for this operation to be successful. Even if Mulcahy and Dieter were in this together, Sam had no idea how large an adversary his people would be going up against. Coordinating everyone was of the utmost importance. Sam was sure that Commander Thomas would be activating all the hidden weaponry in Bridgeport and Stratford, on standby alert, to close down any escape routes the enemy might attempt to use. He almost forgot that Martha was going to call regarding Mulcahy.

❋   ❋   ❋

"Mulcahy's family made their fortune running liquor, along with some of the big Irish families of Boston," Martha began. "These people are no strangers to violence and murder. They are known to go after whatever they want, by whatever means necessary. They have no problem with killing their enemies. Strangely, some of these families actually are known sympathizers with the German cause. Sam, I believe these people are connected with the Illuminati. They have participated in many student rallies, and have incited riots on some of the college campuses up in Boston. I'm sure they feel that Hitler is going to win this war, and if that happens, he would need sympathizers here to run the country for him. I'm guessing these people believe they will be the people put in charge. This is really sick, Sam. These people are Americans. How can they be part of such a thing as this?"

"Power and arrogance," said Sam. "They believe the country has taken a wrong turn, and it needs them to set it back on a right course, whatever that is. They believe they will have amazing power and must be stopped. I believe they are going to strike tonight. Everything points to it. I need you to stay strong. Don't tell the family anything about this. If all goes well, there won't be any need. If it doesn't, please take care of our family. I know this may be overwhelming right now, but I'm counting on you to do this. I know you can. Promise me you'll stay strong."

Martha's response was stunned silence. She had to stop the tears that were welling up in her eyes. She could hardly believe what she was hearing. She hadn't even been a Tyler for six months, and was now facing the possibility of having to become head of the family.

"Martha, are you there?" Sam asked.

"Yes, Sam, I'm here," said Martha.

"Come on, Honey, we're going to get through this. Our country needs us," said Sam.

They said their goodbyes, and told each other of their love. Now it was time to take on some Nazis.

CHAPTER THIRTY

A Coast Guard launch was sent to collect everyone. At 3 PM everyone involved was sitting around a large conference table at the secret command post, beneath the Villa Rosa. No one in Bridgeport was aware of its presence. The plan was relatively simple. The Navy would be bringing in marine sharpshooters by way of the Brooklyn Navy Yard. They would deploy with the Bridgeport police. Their job was to seal off the harbor once the intruders came onto land. The sharpshooters would be placed in the high places to give them plenty of clear vantage points. Searchlights had been set in place so that anyone near the tank in any direction, would be denied the cover of darkness. They would be totally exposed by the lights. The plan was to let the enemy in, and make sure they could not get back out. Of course, the main objective was to make sure they could not place any explosives near the tank.

The Coast Guard cutter would be keeping an eye on three tankers scheduled to drop anchor off New Haven Harbor. It was a safe bet one of them would be carrying the group of men charged with carrying out their mission. The Bridgeport Fire Department had bomb specialists. Their's would be the job of defusing any bombs should they be activated. The Milford Police would be with Sam, patrolling Charles Island. Sam was convinced that there was at least one area in the tunnels that was not discovered by the local police and could be used as a command center. He told officer Perkins to report anything suspicious in the water, to the Coast Guard. They would dispatch helicopters from Bridgeport and the Navy gunship, keeping a low profile off Penfield Reef, in Fairfield, just beyond the Bridgeport city line, at the end of Seaside Park.

Sam's plan was to pretty much create what is known as a gauntlet. It allows an alleyway for any intruder to gain entrance, and then closes once the intruder is inside. All that remained now was for it to become dark enough for the enemy to feel safe. That would not occur until at least 9 o' clock.

As a precaution, Sam decided to pull the New Haven police into the plan. He knew Matt D'Onofrio was not anxious to be left out of the action. Once the fireworks began, they were to board whatever tankers were docked in New Haven Harbor, and all access to the Sound was to be cut off.

Commander Thomas was impressed by the plan. As he saw it, that left very little chance for the Germans to succeed. Of course, he was a military man and was not used to taking orders from a civilian. He was poised to pull out all the stops if things did not go well. The Coast Guard gunship would do much damage to the tankers; and the fighter planes in the hangers, in Bridgeport and in New Haven, could devastate anything that came their way. The Coast Guard had boats and aircraft on the ocean side of Long Island. For anyone attempting an attack from there, it would be a suicide mission. Sam was sure that the enemy was aware of the risks and would probably be more than ready to take them. This was not going to be a picnic. Everyone involved was about to get a very real taste of what war is all about.

※   ※   ※

Matt took Sam, Commander Thomas and Officer Perkins to Consiglio's on Wooster Street. He was convinced that a good old Italian meal was just with the group needed to fortify themselves for the evening's festivities. The four men were surprisingly comfortable in each other's company. They ate their meal, went over the plan a few more times, then went to their respective posts to wait for nightfall.

※   ※   ※

Martha did exactly what Sam had asked her not to do. As soon as she got home, she took Aunt Clara aside and told her all that was happening, and just how dangerous Sam's responsibilities were. She reasoned that if anything bad should happen to Sam, it would be hard for her and Aunt Clara to exist with each other. Besides, she and Aunt Clara had become so close that she knew there was no way she could hide the truth from her, not even for a few hours. And to be totally honest, she didn't want to. In her mind, there was no way to justify keeping this wonderful woman, who had done so much for Sam and the children, in the dark. Martha knew Sam was only trying to do the right thing, but Aunt Clara had become too precious to her to lose, if Sam were lost. It was an enormous decision to make, but that's the one she made; she was sure she made the right one.

Aunt Clara totally agreed. The news stunned her, momentarily. The thought of losing Sam was too awful to contemplate. She grabbed Martha and hugged her tight.

"I'm so glad Sam found you," she said. "You're just what this family needs."

Just then, Ella Mae Rucker came through the door. She had just finished cleaning, over at Martha and Sam's place.

"Is Henry picking you up soon?" Aunt Clara asked.

"Any time now," said Ella Mae.

"Well, tell him to wait, Woman. We have work to do," said Aunt Clara, who went out on the porch and called to Injun Jim.

"Take the children up to Zuckerman's. Give them whatever they want, then bring them back and tell them one of your stories, you hear?"

"Yes, ma'am," said Injun Jim. "But . . . ."

"'But' nothing, Mister," she cut him off.

Injun Jim just shrugged and did as he was told. The children squealed with delight.

Just then, Henry Rucker pulled his Chevy into Aunt Clara's driveway.

"Henry, you wait right here. We need Ella Mae to come pray with us," said Aunt Clara.

Henry said nothing. He lowered the back of his seat, leaned back, closed his eyes, folded his arms, and wore a big smile on his face.

Aunt Clara took Martha and Ella Mae in tow, and proceeded up Main Street to Saint Peter's. She and the ladies had some serious praying to do.

CHAPTER THIRTY-ONE

It was 9:30 PM, and the moon forgot to come out. It was the darkest night Sam could remember.

"Oh, perfect," he muttered. "Just what I need. This isn't going to be difficult enough? Just whose side is nature on?" he wondered. Sam realized he had to break this sour mood, but he wasn't happy about it.

The Coast Guard cutter was anchored miles offshore. Sam had a sailor with him to signal the cutter so that it, in turn, could signal all the other groups waiting for the Germans to act. There was a lot of tension in the air. Every man knew exactly how important his part was. To fail would bring horrific consequences. At 11 o'clock, five men emerged from the water, 50 feet from the giant tank. Everyone had expected them to make their approach using some sort of amphibious craft. Score one surprise for the enemy. The intruders quickly made their way to their target. Two of the men were carrying a large, soft cover equipment bag. The man in charge issued his directives. Each man took his equipment consisting of a handgun, wires, and heavy magnetic plates to secure the explosives, and went to attach them to their section at the base of the tank. They set up about 15 feet apart.

Suddenly, they were surprised by the blinding illumination of the many huge search lamps furnished by the Bridgeport police department. A voice boomed out for them to stop what they were doing and raise their hands. The plan was to have the sharpshooters get them before they could use the bombs as a defense. Foolishly, some of the Germans went for their weapons. It was a bad decision. Within seconds, all five men were mortally wounded in a blistering hail of gunfire. The officer in charge sent a squad of police with the bomb people, to get control of the explosives and to make sure none had been deployed. Once the police made sure that all five men were dead, they had the bodies taken to the morgue. For the next half hour they made an exhaustive search to make sure no explosives had been overlooked.

The Coast Guard vessel signaled to Sam's position what had happened in Bridgeport. But, for Sam, the night had just begun. It was now his turn to get in on the action. He was about to get into the Milford police boat, when Perkins came running down the dock.

"Just got a call from the cops and Bridgeport. The five men they killed all had wet suits and came up out of the water. Sam, there has to be a boat somewhere over there. I wouldn't be surprised if someone got them close and was going to bring them back to wherever they started out from," said Perkins.

"Got any ideas?" Sam asked.

"Yeah, a good bet would be the rental cottages on Pleasure Beach in Bridgeport, right across from Short Beach in Stratford. No one thought about that place.

"Let's take care of first things first. Keep your eyes peeled. If Charles Island is where this all started, then Charles Island is where it is all going to end. I'll take four officers with me now. You go and get as many as you can round up, and meet me out there," said Sam.

Perkins hightailed it out to get his car, and got on his radio to the dispatcher. He told him to have every available officer meet him at the harbor, immediately. They were to consider this a state of emergency. Within ten minutes, five more officers appeared and joined Perkins in the harbormaster's boat, headed out towards Charles Island. Sam gathered everyone and deployed them around the island.

"I'll take two men in with me," Sam told Perkins. "You take the rest and spread out over the southern exposure. If anyone tries to come back this way, deal with them. Don't take any chances; these people will be desperate. I'm pretty sure Dieter did not die with that group in Bridgeport. It's a good bet he's on his way back here. If anything goes wrong for me, you are in charge. Don't let any of them get away. If you have any doubts, shoot first."

Perkins nodded affirmatively. He knew exactly what Sam was about to do and he did not like the fact that he was not going to go into the tunnels with him. Sam was sure that there was a secret room off one of the tunnel walls. He was hoping that Mulcahy was down there. It was time for someone to pay for Caroline's death.

❋   ❋   ❋

Sam and the two officers brought flashlights and torches to light the way and the sconces. He led the men down the back stairwell to the basement, and over to the storage case that gave way to the tunnel passage. Sam motioned for the men to go slowly and with extreme caution. He was sure the secret room had to be accessed by one of the rooms off the tunnel. They moved deliberately and cautiously.

As they got to the third room, Sam was sure that he saw a flicker of light coming from under a wall. It was only for a split second. He noticed a sconce on the wall with a thick metal plate attached to it. He turned and told the men to stop, and motioned for them to be quiet. He went back out into the tunnel and observed two other sconces attached to the walls. They too had metal braces, but theirs were much thinner and more of a decorative type. He would've noticed that on the walls of the first two rooms; he hadn't. He was now sure that the one in this room was there to allow someone to pull the wall open. He turned and spoke to the officers.

"Let's go. Let's work our way down the tunnels. There's got to be a room down here somewhere. Check every room carefully."

Sam motioned for the men to go left out of the room. He would go to the right. They exited the room. Sam went about ten feet down the hallway, and then turned around and dropped down on one knee, pulled out his service revolver and waited. After a short wait, he was sure he heard movement from inside the room. He was right. A tall thin man eased his way into the hallway. His back was to Sam. He was looking down the tunnel in the direction of the officers.

"Mulcahy," said Sam.

The man stopped, frozen in his tracks.

"It's all over, Mulcahy. Drop your weapon, raise your hands, and turn around."

"I should have known you would figure this out, Tyler," said Mulcahy. "There is only one way for me to go. I'll be branded a traitor and they will execute me. My only hope is to get past you, and make it out of here."

"That's not going to happen," said Sam.

"I have to try, Captain. You must understand, I have no choice."

"You do, Mulcahy. Come peacefully, and stop all this bloodshed," said Sam.

"Sorry, captain," said Mulcahy as he whirled around towards Sam. He was ready to fire when he realized Sam was down on one knee. He tried to make the adjustment in his aim to fire, but was met by two rounds from Sam's weapon, which struck him in the chest. Mulcahy fell against the wall and stumbled backwards to his left. He was met by two more rounds, fired off by one of the officers who had come back that way when he heard all the noise. Sam went over to check to see if Mulcahy was dead.

Mulcahy grabbed hold of his pants leg and hissed, "Heil Hitler," with his last breath.

"Don't shoot," came a voice from the room. A smallish man, in his early fifties, came out with his hands in the air.

"Don't shoot me," he yelled.

"Cuff him," said Sam to one of the officers. "Let's get out of here and join the others. Take this guy to the boat and stay with him. You come with me," he said to the other, the one who shot Mulcahy.

No sooner had Sam and the officer gotten out of the building, they heard the sound of gunfire coming from where Perkins and his men were deployed. They made their way over to Perkins' position.

"One guy with a lot of firepower," was Perkins' response to Sam's question.

"It's got to be Dieter," said Sam. "Get every man, and keep a ten foot space, and let's work our way north. The group worked their way to the far shore. Dieter was nowhere to be found.

"Break off in groups of two," said Sam, "and canvas the whole island. Lights on; let's go."

All the officers began to search the island. Sam went over to the boat Dieter used to get there.

"Disable the motor," he told the officer, who immediately separated the motor from the craft and threw it into the water.

"No one will be using that one," said the officer.

The officer then took the lead position with Sam following closely behind. The man was a hunter and moved very quietly through the brush. Suddenly, a shot rang out from the right, striking the officer in his right arm. Sam saw the flash from Dieter's gun and now knew where he was.

"It barely hit me, Captain," said the officer. "Go get him, Sir."

Sam worked his way towards Dieter's position, exchanging fire as he went. Finally, Dieter was out of bullets. He came out from behind the tree he was using for cover, and threw his weapon to the ground.

"You wouldn't shoot an unarmed man, Captain, would you?" Dieter asked.

"Why did you kill that young woman in South Carolina?" Sam asked.

"Your cousin?" Dieter said.

"You knew that?" Sam asked.

"Of course I did. Kempler tried to bargain with me by using her to prevent me from killing him. He foolishly believed that the knowledge that the girl's cousin was a state police captain would scare me off. I came here to blow up America. No policeman was going to stand in my way. Kempler left me no choice. I had to deal with him, and get back here as quickly as possible. Unfortunately, the girl was in the way. It's a shame she had to suffer the same fate as Kempler; and believe me, she suffered.

A look of surprise came over Dieter's face as he witnessed Sam lowering his weapon and letting it fall to the ground.

"That was a mistake, Captain," said Dieter.

Sam had been hoping for something like this to happen ever since he got word of how Caroline had died. He had played the scenario over and over in his head. Then a smile of satisfaction came over his face.

"Believe me, Mister, you are going to wish I had shot you," came Sam's smug retort.

Dieter moved cautiously towards Sam's position. He was a very powerful man and was convinced that if he could get his hands on Sam, he would be able to render him defenseless. Sam hardly moved, showing no defensive posture. Dieter lunged forward, only to be met by two very hard and lightning quick left jabs to his face, that stung more than Dieter wanted to admit. His eyes momentarily watered. As he reached up to clear his eyes, Sam moved in and landed two powerful kidney punches. Dieter winced. Sam struck him with a left to his jaw, a powerful right to his stomach, and then a right uppercut to the jaw that sent him flying backwards, hitting the ground with a lot of pain. Slowly, Dieter got to his feet. Sam moved quickly forward, but stopped abruptly, as Dieter shot his right leg out to kick him. Sam had anticipated the move. He grabbed Dieter's extended leg and sent a crushing kick to his left knee, sending Dieter howling to the ground in pain. As Dieter looked up, he was met with two very hard blows to the face. By now, Dieter's face was covered in his own blood.

"You're going to die, Dieter, but it won't hurt as much as this will. You tortured my poor cousin; and now I'm going to torture you. Your only hope is for someone to come and prevent it. Now, get up!" Sam ordered.

With a great deal of effort, Dieter got to his feet. It took some time. He would wish that he hadn't. Sam moved in and landed a right and left to his face. Each blow snapped his head back. By now, Sam's clothes were beginning to be covered with Dieter's blood. Dieter was using all the power he could muster to stand. Sam grabbed him by the neck and threw him to the ground.

"This is your lucky day," said Sam. "You are about to be rescued by the United States of America. We'll dress your wounds, see that you heal, and then we'll execute you. Whatever happens to your fatherland, you won't be around to see it. And guess what, pal—you failed!"

As the rest of the officers came on the scene, Sam gave orders for the signal man to signal the Coast Guard cutter, to board and search the one tanker anchored off New Haven, to see if it was carrying Germans. D'Onofrio got the word, and with thirty police officers from the New Haven police department, boarded both tankers and arrested five more Germans.

The mission was a smashing success. Bridgeport Harbor was secure; Mulcahy was dead, and Wilhelm Dieter, their hatchet man, was taken into custody. Everyone involved with the German plot was either dead, or in the hands of the United States Government.

Commander Thomas came with the Coast Guard cutter to pick up the marine sharpshooters. Thomas gave the officer in charge of the Bridgeport mission his orders, then returned to his boat and headed out to Charles Island to meet up with Sam. Two marines put a very badly beaten Wilhelm Dieter and the mystery man from the tunnels, aboard the Coast Guard cutter, with Sam and Commander Thomas to meet up with D'Onofrio, at

New Haven Harbor. But not before Sam thanked Officer Perkins for all his help, and told him how grateful he was for all that he did. Sam didn't know it, but his handling of Officer Perkins gained him a new friend and a very valuable and capable ally down in Milford, should Sam ever need one.

CHAPTER THIRTY-TWO

Matt D'Onofrio was waiting at New Haven Harbor, as the launch from the Coast Guard cutter brought Sam, Commander Thomas, and their prisoners ashore. D'Onofrio took one look at Dieter and started to laugh.

"You do that?" D'Onofrio asked Sam.

Sam smiled, and answered, "Yes. Yes I did."

"You didn't, by any chance, warn him that you were a three-time state of Connecticut amateur boxing champ did you?" D'Onofrio asked.

"I knew I forgot something," said Sam.

Once again, D'Onofrio looked at Dieter who was having a very difficult time standing. He then looked back at Sam. "Nice job," he deadpanned.

"We do what we can," Sam assured him.

"I have been ordered by the Army to take these prisoners into custody, over to New Haven. The Army is sending a prisoner transport, as we speak. The governor wants them out of Connecticut, as fast as possible. There is a Lieutenant Colonel, stationed at Yale, to transport them to Fort Dix, over in New Jersey. It might take a few days, but I'm sure the boys down in Dix will get all the information we need to know from these two. I'm sure the ones we got on the tanker are not anything more than goons. Doesn't look to me like there is one whole brain in the bunch."

Sam, Matt, and the commander went over to police headquarters to meet the Army Colonel. All three made their reports to the Colonel. The man in the tunnel turned out to be Charles Gardner, a professor emeritus of chemistry at MIT, who was on sabbatical. Mulcahy duped him into putting the explosives together, with a system to detonate them from a safe distance. Gardner was a widower who had no children and very little family or friends. He was the perfect fit for Mulcahy's plans. No one would miss him. It would be the Army's responsibility to see if he was telling the truth. Both Sam and Matt were inclined to believe his story. The man had a spotless record. In fact, he had no record at all. He was known as a loner; a ghost, really. It was late, but all available intelligence tended to exonerate him. Of course, the military would take its sweet time doing that. They really could not be faulted. National security was definitely at stake, and no one wanted to be guilty of sloppy investigative work. As for Gardner, it was just a case of being the wrong guy, in the wrong place, at the wrong time, with the wrong people.

It was 3 o'clock in the morning, time for everyone to head out. Sam had put in a call to Martha around 1:30. Martha and Aunt Clara danced and hugged all around the kitchen. Ella Mae had stayed to spend the night with the children, while Martha and Aunt Clara continued their vigil. Martha told Sam she would be waiting for him on the patio. Sam liked the sound of that.

❋   ❋   ❋

The kitchen table at Aunt Clara's was alive with joy, and no small amount of relief. Sam had to be back at the barracks, but managed to push the time of arrival back to 10 o'clock. The children were already at school, still none the wiser of what a hero their father was.

Martha had an 11 o'clock lecture. It was going to be a lot easier for her, now that Sam was safe and the whole affair was finally over. As she walked across the lawn to her home, she started giving some thought as to how short a time she had been here in Wolf Harbor, and how she and Sam had already been through two harrowing experiences. She wondered if their life was always going to be like this.

"Well, it sure won't be boring," she reasoned.

Martha went through the kitchen and into the living room, heading towards the stairs leading to the second floor. Something told her she was not alone. She stopped and turned to see Allison Tinsley standing there. Allison had a gun. It looked like a .38 caliber Smith and Wesson.

"Why are you here, Allison?" Martha asked.

"You have taken everything from me," Allison said.

"Are you involved in all of this?" Martha asked.

"What do you think?" Allison returned.

"But your father . . . Are you the one who placed those notes from Dieter to your father?" Martha asked.

"You're darn right I did. My father, my father, that silly milk toast fool. My mother couldn't stand him; he turned her stomach. And then she deserted us, and left me with him. My life has been nauseating. I knew exactly what Mulcahy was up to. After the Germans had won, Lawrence and his family would have great power here, and I would finally be free of that fool of a father. I would have wealth and power. But now, thanks to Sam, all of that is gone. I knew when Lawrence didn't return last night that he failed and was probably dead. It's all over the news on the radio this morning. Now I have nothing."

"Killing me won't get Sam back for you" said Martha.

"Sam? That's not what this is all about. I don't want Sam. I want to hurt Sam, just like I have been hurt. I want Sam to feel the pain of loss, just like I do. I want Sam's life to be just as miserable as mine is. That's what I want for Sam; and killing you is just how I'm going to make that happen," said Allison.

Martha knew that she had to get closer to Allison if she were to have any chance of getting the gun from her. She could see that Allison was very fit. Allison had been an athlete in high school and college. Martha also knew a woman's fury was, indeed, something to be reckoned with. She took a step towards Allison. Surprisingly, Allison took a step forward herself, drastically cutting down the distance between them.

"What do you think you're doing?" Allison hissed, as she pointed her weapon directly at Martha.

Martha didn't respond, but looked over Allison's shoulder as if she were looking at someone. Allison cocked her weapon, but did not take a step back. Instead, she cautiously looked back over her shoulder. It was just enough for Martha to make her move. Martha lunged for the gun and grabbed Allison's gun hand with both hands. Her assessment of Allison's strength was correct—she was strong. But Martha had studied judo with much bigger men. She used Allison's movements to rock her arm back and forth. Suddenly, the gun went off. Neither woman quit the struggle.

"Was that a gunshot?" Aunt Clara asked Sam, who quickly got up and went out onto the porch.

Once again the gun discharged, and this time Martha felt an advantage. She twisted Allison's arm and then flipped her over onto her back. The gun flew out of Allison's hand, but the fall did not stop her. She quickly rose to her feet, and charged for the gun. Sam and Aunt Clara started running across the lawn. Allison had just reached for the gun as Martha used her right foot to kick her in the side, sending her headlong into the stone fireplace. Allison held her head and felt the blood running down her face. With a loud scream she rushed towards Martha who caught her with both hands while falling backwards, with her foot planted in Allison's stomach. She flipped her high into the air, sending her crashing to the floor with a mighty thud. Martha quickly got to her feet. Allison rolled over, moaning in pain. Slowly, she got to her feet, only to be met with a crushing right fist to her jaw, compliments of one very angry Martha Tyler. Allison sank to the floor in a heap.

Sam and Aunt Clara ran into the living room just in time to see Martha lift Allison to her feet, holding her hair with one hand and locking Allison's arm tightly behind her back with the other.

"There is a gun over there," Martha told Sam, pointing to the stone fireplace.

Sam retrieved the gun, and placed handcuffs on Allison's wrists.

"Ezra Tinsley is innocent. She and Mulcahy framed him. I'll fill you in later. But now, take this pathetic person out of our house!"

Sam called the local police and had them take Allison into custody, until the Army could come and take charge of her. He knew that this was the final piece of the puzzle. All of a sudden, a peace came over his whole body. He looked approvingly over to his wife.

"You really are something, aren't you?"

EPILOGUE

Newspaper headlines across the country trumpeted the exploits of the Connecticut State Police Captain who thwarted a major Nazi espionage attempt on American lives, here on the home front. Martha could not believe the amazing turn of events that sent her from New York and desperation, to the arms of a national hero who married her and gave her a wonderful family, and life beyond her wildest dreams.

As the train slowed down, approaching the Old Saybrook train station, the crowd waiting to greet the family began to cheer wildly. Sam had been decorated by the President of the United States, in the Rose Garden at the White House, with his family in attendance. Now, Martha, Sam and the family were about to spend an afternoon of celebration on the town green in Essex, with all their friends and neighbors.

It was good to see all the townspeople sharing a time of joy, and even for a short time, a welcome escape from thoughts of the war and all the havoc it had brought with it. Sam was now the new toast of the town, a mantle he was most uncomfortable with. After the last good-bye and hearty handshake, Sam and the family had dinner with Aunt Clara, then took the children home and tucked them into bed.

Martha and Sam sat on their front porch enjoying the warm sea breezes and unobstructed view of the moon over Wolf Harbor. Sam got up to answer the phone. He was on 24-hour call, so he assumed the call was for him. He was right. Chief White was calling from Columbia. The chief relayed that he had wondered just how anyone could have known Kempler was in South Carolina. He wanted to make sure his area was not infiltrated by any Germans. The answer to this, and all of his questions, came up with Allison Tinsley's name written all over them.

Allison knew that Sam and his family were going to Washington, on their way to South Carolina. She sent the Illuminati tip at Mulcahay's request, to try to throw suspicion on the Skull and Bones. Allison had heard Caroline talking about the new mystery man in her life. The man Caroline described sounded very much like Kempler. She passed the information on to Mulcahy, who contacted some associates near Sumter. They confirmed Kempler's presence and passed the word back to Mulcahy, who immediately dispatched Dieter to go there and kill him. Mulcahy's associates were arrested and found not only to be sympathizers, but part of a group giving aid to the Nazi cause. They, too, were Illuminati believers who were very much in favor of overthrowing the government.

The FBI was most grateful to Chief White for involving them, as they were able to take a few bows for their efforts. Army intelligence was happy because the FBI had given them Allison Tinsley, who, they came to realize, was at the center of much of the conspiracy. Poor Allison—she was so disillusioned by her life that she was completely taken in by Mulcahy and his people. All the Tinsley money in the world was not going to keep her from the executioner's hand.

Sam walked back out to the porch and rejoined Martha. He told her all that Chief White had said.

"Finally," she thought," Sam and I can spend a night just enjoying each other's company without thoughts of war and murder ever on our minds. That was, for tonight. Tomorrow, Martha would be busy beginning work on her next book, the further adventures of the Tylers of Wolf Harbor.

As for Sam, he was content just to have one night of peace and solitude. Sam was a police officer. Not for one moment did he allow himself to think of peace beyond the present day. There was a war going on, and there was always someone out there ready to commit a crime. For tonight, all was good.

But for tomorrow?

The End

Edwards Brothers, Inc.
Thorofare, NJ USA
August 29, 2011